POISONED KISSES

MANDY ROSKO

1

Consistently being caught up in some evil scientist's plot to experiment on people wasn't something John thought he'd ever get wrapped up in.

Again and again and again.

The leather straps digging into John's wrists and throat were nothing compared to the scratchy, itchy feeling of Bobby's gross hairs and mandibles against his face and shoulders.

"He told me not to bite you. I might give you a little something anyway. He won't have to know."

Jesus Christ. John was so happy he was high off his ass on whatever meds he'd been pumped with. Otherwise, that creepy fucker would've had him screaming and thrashing on the table.

He was awake and aware enough to be grateful for that much.

That he didn't have to lie here looking like a little bitch, crying about being locked up all over again.

Bobby pulled back just enough, grabbing a fistful of John's hair, to meet his eyes.

The man's face looked worse by the day.

His mandibles stretched out his cheeks. Long, sharp, and coarse hairs poked out of his mouth and lips.

Tarantulas had hairs like that, didn't they? They shot them from their asses at predators to confuse them and escape.

Itched like a bitch. Everywhere Bobby touched him with them, he wanted to scratch.

The straps prevented that.

John couldn't shift, either. It was as though his inner cobra was behind a wall in his mind. Close, but so far away.

"Don't like looking at it?" Bobby slurred, his gaze wild, a little vein bulging at the corner of his right eye. "*You* fucking did this."

Technically, Mother had done it, and Bobby had signed up for it while John only sat back and watched. Did he say that out loud? He didn't think so, but the next thing he knew, a harsh, dull pressure landed on his face, again and again and again.

Bobby was punching him.

Yeah, these drugs are amazing.

More screaming from Bobby, more shouting. It sounded so far away, muffled, as though John's ears were clogged with pillows made of thick cotton and feathers.

When he finally came-to once again, the first thing he noticed was that his whole body felt cold and wet. Sweat. He was sweating. Made sense.

Then, he opened his eyes and realized that someone new was in the room with him. At least it wasn't Bobby's ugly face inches in front of his own anymore.

Now, concerned green eyes stared down at him from their place on a pretty face, just above a pointed nose dusted with freckles.

She smiled at him, though there was nothing happy in it. "H-hey, there you are. You're okay now."

She wiped something soft down the side of his face. A cool rag. He kept right on shivering, not taking his eyes off her.

"You're wasting your time," Bobby said. He apparently hadn't left. "Guy doesn't know where he is or what's going on."

"Then you should stop hurting him," the green-eyed woman snapped.

At first, John thought she was wearing a bright red dress. No, he squinted hard and focused. That was her hair hanging around her shoulders. Bright red, like a fire truck or a juicy apple.

His arms twitched, but he couldn't reach up and touch her tresses. At first, he was confused, but then he remembered straps were holding his wrists down.

The woman wiped the sweat from John's neck. He didn't feel much of the cold anymore, but her touch felt warm.

"Like he can tell," Bobby slurred. "Fucker deserves it anyway."

The woman's expression on her round face turned sour. She glared back at Bobby. "Will you go away already?"

"Why?" Bobby asked, stepping forward, now into John's view.

John didn't like that. He growled at the man.

Bobby paid no attention to him. He was taller than the red-haired woman, and the more John's thoughts cleared up, the more sure of himself he was that the ugly bastard was using his fucked-up face to make the woman uncomfortable, too.

"You want to make nice with him because you feel bad? He did this to me." Bobby pointed at his face, his mandibles shivering and the long, pointed hairs twitching. "He'd do it to you, too."

John wouldn't though. And he really hadn't been the one to do it to Bobby, either. He'd only been an observer.

"You... agreed to it." John struggled to get the words out. He had to defend himself a little here, even if he wasn't sure how much of what was being said was real.

The woman looked down at him. Bobby's eyes flared like he was about to fly off the deep end.

He surged forward, his clawed hands reaching for John's neck.

"Stop it! Stop it!" The woman stepped in the way, her smaller body shielding John, pushing back against Bobby before he could strangle John.

Sink his claws into John's throat and kill him.

She shoved Bobby back, but it was clearly not done under her own strength. Bobby stopped because he wanted to, sneering at the woman.

"Daddy's little girl, protecting others now? Stupid bitch. You're just taken in because he likes things that are pretty to look at." Bobby stepped closer, making the woman cringe when he touched her red hair. "If he hadn't done this to my face, I wonder if you'd look at me the same."

The woman slapped his hand away. "No."

"Why? What makes him different from me? Other than I look like a monster?"

"You talk like a creep, that's why."

That seemed to be the wrong thing to say. Bobby's cheeks, the parts of them that John could see through the stretching of his lips and the long, tarantula hairs coming out of his mouth, turned a bright shade of red.

Bobby raised his hand, as if to slap her.

John hissed at him, his own cobra fangs coming out long and sharp and dripping with poison.

The woman jumped away from him, her gasp cutting the air.

"That's fucking pathetic, but whatever, fine." Bobby didn't move. He didn't look smug or triumphant either. He did turn his nose up at John for it though. "Just make sure not to touch him. He might poison you."

"I wasn't touching him," the woman replied, holding her hands together, now looking as though John was the one she feared in the room.

"Not even with that rag," Bobby insisted. "Your precious *Daddy* wouldn't like it. And don't let yourself feel bad for him. Don't forget that this snake would do this to you, too, if you let him."

"N-no." He wouldn't. John swore he *wouldn't*. He tried to say as much, deny it further, but his tongue was suddenly so thick he couldn't get any more words out.

The poison. In his mouth. *Fuck*. His whole mouth was getting swollen because he'd forgotten to take care when he let his fangs out.

He could still poison himself if he wasn't careful.

Luckily, it wasn't enough poison to completely close off his throat, but he was woozy all over again, helpless as Bobby stepped closer to the red-haired woman.

To her credit, she stood with her back straight, staring up at him with as much courage as she could muster. Until Bobby surged forward and back in a fake-out, making her jump.

Bobby laughed, his hands on his belly, his mandibles spread wide. John had never seen the guy look so happy about anything before in his life as he walked off.

The woman stood where she was, a slight tremble in her

bare arms. She looked so frail. That green dress, if it could be called that, hung off her body like a potato sack.

"Asshole," she muttered, as though afraid Bobby would hear it. Then she looked back at John, catching his eyes.

John lay where he was. He didn't have the strength to get up, to lift his head even if he hadn't been strapped down.

His throat felt hot and swollen and not because of the poison he'd swallowed. He was just tired.

The woman came closer, carrying herself with more caution this time. She grabbed the rag she'd been using to clean his face of grime and sweat. She didn't apply it to his cheek this time, though he wished she would.

He wanted more of that touch.

"Is it true your skin is poison?"

He couldn't have heard that right. His *skin*? All of it? Poison?

He tried to shake his head, but again, the straps that held him down wouldn't allow it. All he could do was gaze upon her.

The woman was beautiful, in a pale, ghostly sort of way. And she smelled like flowers.

"Who did this to you? Bobby?" Her gentle, barely-there caress with the cloth on his face stung the still healing cuts. Injuries from an owl's claws.

John hissed. His tongue felt thick and heavy and dry in his mouth.

Her shoulders sagged. She tossed the cloth away. Into the trash? He still couldn't be sure. It was hard to see.

"Do you want some water?"

"Y...es," he croaked, and then he moaned when he felt a straw touch his lips.

God, water was good.

Then she was gone again, and he struggled to focus. He

wanted so much to have her close, if only because she was the only soft touch he'd received since he'd woken up down here.

He wished he could tell her, wished he could plead his innocence. But she was right to suspect him. Smart, too. Why should she believe he was innocent? Bobby had a point. The woman was being stupidly kind, and she was going to take pity on the wrong person one day.

Someone who would take advantage of that kindness. Use it against her and hurt her.

A shadow approached her from behind. John thought it was the lights playing tricks on him again. He tried to move. Tried to warn her, but he couldn't.

She let out a small shriek, which was cut off quickly when the huge male spun her around, putting at least five more feet between them.

"What are you doing down here?" The voice was deep and gruff. Sounded familiar. Maybe something John had heard while still mostly put under.

"I... I'm sorry, Matt—"

"Don't say my name in front of him."

"I'm sorry." She glanced back at John, her pink lips snapping shut.

The new man grunted. He didn't look much older than her. Maybe early twenties or so. Her lover? John clenched his hands.

"He seems out of it. He might not have caught that. What are you doing here?"

"I just... I wanted to see?" The woman curled in on herself, her hand gripping her arm. Like she feared getting a slap or a hit.

The guy was tall, broad in the shoulders, and bigger than John was by a mile even when he was at his peak.

John didn't like that. Didn't trust this guy, but at least the new arrival didn't strike the woman.

"We're not supposed to see." His deep, booming voice softened. "This isn't for us."

A lover then. Well, it wasn't like John was going to have a chance at anything here anyway, but being tied down to a metal table with nothing nice to look at but the leaky pipes in the ceiling...

She'd made for a nice little fantasy.

"Where did the scars on his face come from?"

"Some fight, probably. Come. We should go." Matt gently took her hand, pulling her farther away from John's table. And God, John felt so fucking lonely. He'd even take Bobby's company right about then.

"He's poisonous to the touch. Look what he did to himself."

"I see."

"Did you touch him?"

"With a rag, but not skin to skin."

The big man grunted. "You're not wearing gloves. Come and wash your hands." He pulled her toward a big, metal sink that John could only make out from the corner of his eye.

The water ran. They spoke about something. A mention of "father." Ah. So they were siblings.

Strange, they looked nothing alike.

Was their father the fox shifter? John vaguely remembered the man who'd instructed Bobby to jump John and pull the black bag over his head.

Had to be. That guy seemed so... in charge.

"Matt, not that one," the woman said softly.

"It's the yellow one," he replied.

"It's not. Look at the label. See this skull? That's not the soap we use."

John glanced over, as much as he could, still only able to see from his peripheral vision with the damned strap around his throat.

The big guy stared dumbly at the bottle. "We use this for cleaning, though."

"Cleaning, not washing hands. This is poison as well. This will burn us."

"Oh." He sounded ashamed.

"It's all right," the red-haired woman quickly said. "I tell him he shouldn't move things out of their original bottles. See this one here? This is the regular soap."

"For dishes and hands."

"Yes, see these letters?" She went over it with him, her voice gentle and patient.

John started to wonder, could this guy not read or something?

He seemed unhappy as the red-haired woman went over the symbols and words on the bottle with him.

Turns out, he *could* read. Just slowly. The smaller words he picked up on well enough. The larger words he sounded out, like a child.

Okay. Interesting.

They washed their hands together before moving toward the metal door leading out of the room. John pulled against the straps. He must have made a noise because they stopped to look back at him.

The woman looked right at him, meeting his eyes, and John had a split second of clarity in his vision.

She had freckles across her nose and cheeks and forehead. Eyes so wide and green and bright they reminded him of the foliage and trees he used to slither through.

It was like she stood under a spotlight, a glow casting through her red hair like fire.

She was so fucking beautiful.

Matt put his hand on the woman's shoulder. "Bobby is right. He isn't always right, but this time he is. This man is dangerous. Don't feel bad for him."

"O-okay," she said, her voice small. "Are they planning on hurting him more than he already is?"

That she could be worried for him at all was more than John deserved. This Matt guy was right. John was not to be trusted.

"I have no idea." Matt's mouth set in a firm line. "But I think they're just doing tests for now."

More tests. Christ, was John never going to get away from them?

The woman nodded.

Matt turned out the lights, just for the woman to exclaim, "Don't turn them off!"

"Why?"

"He'll... he'll be alone in the dark."

John closed his eyes, a painful swelling kicking up in his chest. What the hell was such a kind-hearted woman like her doing in a place like this?

"Fine," Matt grunted.

The lights stayed on. The metal door shrieked from a lack of oiling and an over-abundance of rust, and then they were gone.

John wasn't in the dark, but he was alone with his thoughts, and that felt almost just as bad.

His face was still swollen from the owl attack, and his mouth burned from the poison he'd swallowed. He was even pretty sure that Bobby's damned tarantula hairs had gotten into his still-healing wounds, and that made him itch even worse.

John hated everything and everyone.

The boring cells in the FUCN'A—the Furry United Coalition Newbie Academy—facility suddenly seemed like a fever dream, like first-class lodgings compared to this.

John tried to sleep. It wasn't so bad. He knew it was going to get worse long before it got better anyway, so he might as well rest before that fox shifter came back.

Maybe he'd get lucky and that pretty redhead would come to see him again.

Later.

2
_____

Rachel rushed back to her room. If you could call it that. Her space was a corner of the grow room. She liked to call it a greenhouse, even if it was underground and received no natural sunlight.

Her father had said this was the best place for her, and he wasn't wrong. A few sheets, hung ceiling to floor, gave her a small nook all to herself. A feeling of privacy while living in a facility that wasn't made for a family.

It was warm under the specially-made lights. The plants soaked up the rays, and so did Rachel. She so rarely got to go outside, and being here almost made her feel... normal.

Plus, almost everything flowered at some point, so that was nice. Even the potato plants did. When the spuds were under the soil, little lavender flowers came off in clusters along the stems. The tomato plants presented yellow flowers that eventually turned into bulbs that got bigger and redder and became tomatoes. Just like the strawberry plants gave her white petals before the middles turned large and fat and red and delicious.

There was even an apple tree down here, which

somehow managed to bear fruit all year long. She wasn't sure how it managed to do that, but she liked it, snagging a red apple on the way to her corner of the greenhouse.

The flowers were pretty, and she liked taking care of them. And caring for the food. That made her feel useful. It made others look at her like she wasn't just taking up space.

She also couldn't hear too much of everything going on in the rest of the facility in her space.

Everywhere else, it was dark and damp, cold and...scary. She didn't like it. She didn't like that she could hear voices traveling along the pipes. She didn't like that sometimes she could make out the sounds of Bobby's laughter whenever he was making fun of her brother, Matthew, for not being able to read. Or that she sometimes heard that shifter downstairs screaming.

Matthew wasn't going to tell their father where she'd been or what she was doing. He wouldn't, not unless he was forced to. She trusted him like that. Likely, he was going to have another word with Bobby about the things he said and did around here.

How he and the other subjects treated each other.

And John.

Rachel crouched down, pulling her red treasure box out from under her cot. It was an old tackle box she'd found one day on one of her very few trips to the surface. Her father didn't like letting her out. He said he worried for her, and she supposed that made sense. He was her protector. Of course he would worry, but there were also times when he needed her to slink around.

To do some digging, as he called it.

Something about her shifter shape made it easy for her to get around without being noticed. She was a raccoon shifter.

At least, she'd originally thought she was. She'd never seen another raccoon red like her in all the books she'd gotten her hands on until she'd found a page on red pandas. *That* looked much more like her. But her father still told her she was a raccoon. A natural thief.

She'd found the red tackle box when she'd been out on an errand for her father, digging through a dumpster, searching for some papers that seemed to be of great importance. Notes that could not be replaced and would be useful for their family. Some papers had been torn into multiple pieces. Some were in long, thin strips, like confetti, but he'd wanted those, too.

Matthew had been with her, keeping watch, squinting at the papers she'd pulled from the bin.

"What does this say?" he'd asked, pointing when she popped her head out of the bin.

"Oh, it says... Furry United Coalition."

"Oh," he'd said. "What does that mean?"

"I don't know." Rachel had to stop what she was doing and really think about it. "But he wants them, so I guess they're important."

She found the tackle box in the bottom of the dumpster. One of the hinges had been broken off, but it could still close, so she and Matthew had put the papers inside and brought them all back to their father.

He'd been so happy, so proud to see all the papers she'd brought back that he let her keep the tackle box for herself.

Using a knife, she'd scratched some flowers into the red paint, oiled the single hinge that still worked, and now it held her treasures. Sewing supplies, a ballpoint pen and a pencil she'd found discarded in one of the old labs, three sheets of brown paper towel that she could doodle more flowers onto, and a pair of gloves she'd found in one of the bins she'd searched through when she was let above ground.

They'd had holes chewed into them and some of the fingers missing, so she cut all the fingers off and now wore them on the colder nights when they had to conserve power.

There were a few other interesting things she kept in there. A rock she'd found once that looked almost like a misshapen heart. A seagull feather, a pocket mirror, and lipstick she'd found in an abandoned locker.

This facility used to have more people. Her father had said there used to be so many employees here that the halls would be cluttered with them. So many people just wanted to do their work, to study and make medicine. He'd said, back then, the lights were always on and the halls were always clean and sterile.

Not like how it was now. Dark, cold, wet, and... lonely.

Her father knew she had these things, though he didn't approve of her digging around for things that were within the facility. The firm set of his mouth when he'd seen the gloves and the pocket mirror still gave her chills.

He'd slapped her good and hard that day, to the point where Matthew had to step between them. He'd still yelled something fierce before storming out.

He'd visited her later that night though, waking her, pulling her into his lap, stroking her hair, and telling her he was sorry.

"You can't always be taking things, sweetheart. It will get you in trouble."

"I'm sorry." She'd felt so ashamed, weak, and small, as she cried a little.

She was allowed to keep the mirror, the lipstick, and the

gloves, but he warned her to not let her little fingers snatch everything she set her eyes onto.

"Stealing can get you into trouble, sweetheart."

She hadn't understood at the time, still didn't, but she'd asked, "What about ...when I steal from the bins when you ask me to? Is that bad?"

"No," he'd replied.

He hadn't explained further, and Rachel supposed it was none of her business.

Another one of those things he dealt with that he didn't want her troubling herself with.

So much had changed. He always said things were different now from what she could remember. Rachel did know that, out in the real world, away from the facility, people locked up thieves. She was a raccoon shifter. Raccoons were known for stealing, and she was good at it whenever her father sent her out into the world to take things.

She assumed that had to be it. Even as she stroked her papers, her pen, her sewing supplies, and her small rock, she knew thieves weren't good.

Her father was protecting her. The same way he protected all the others.

She pulled out her sewing kit. The little hole at the hem of her dress was opening again. She started to sew it closed. Her father didn't like it when her clothes turned to rags on her. He wanted her to look neat and cleaned up.

A heavy shadow suddenly appeared on the other side of the sheets around her room. She wasn't afraid; she could smell who it was already.

"Give me a minute, Matt. I'm fixing my clothes."

"Our father wants to see you."

She paused.

"Not because of Bobby," he said quickly. "I already talked to him."

She sighed but was not relieved. "You think he'll tell?"

"Probably," Matthew said as Rachel tied off the string and pulled her dress back over her head.

She needed a bra. She didn't have one of those either and was scared to go looking through any more of the abandoned lockers after what happened with the pocket mirror and lipstick.

She pulled aside the curtains and faced her brother, who looked dejected. "Why *did* you have to go and see that snake?"

"I don't know." She ducked her head. That was the thing. She didn't have an answer for that.

He tilted his head. "You were just curious?"

"I guess so," she said. "Can we go?"

Matthew sighed. "You know, I don't like Bobby either…"

"But he's right. We're mean to him because… he looks…"

"That's only half true," Matthew said, shocking Rachel. She'd thought he would deny it. "He's also an asshole."

"Is he, though?" She hadn't been around enough people to really judge.

"Yeah, he is." Matthew shrugged, crossing his big arms over his massive chest, making his T-shirt stretch. "He could be the prettiest-looking guy around here, but I heard what you said about him being a creep before I stepped in. You're right. He is. I'd hate him even if he looked normal."

"Hate is a strong word," Rachel said helplessly.

"That's why I used it," Matthew shot back, just like she knew he would. "Look, anyway the point is that I don't like him, and he doesn't like me, but he is right about the new guy. He's a cobra. He's poisonous, even to himself. That might not be his fault, but I don't want you near him. Understand?"

She didn't understand. It didn't seem fair. The guy didn't look like he was dangerous, but it wasn't his looks she was entirely focused on. She trusted her intuition, her shifter senses, and she felt nothing nefarious around John. Only... sadness.

A deep, penetrating sadness that poured from his eyes.

Sadness, regret, and the sort of emptiness she didn't pick up from Bobby or anyone else. Once in a while, Gerard seemed regretful at times. Lost in thought. But sadness? No, John was the only one who oozed it.

"We let the others walk around," she said petulantly, as if he was the older brother and she the younger sister, instead of her being the older sister.

She was supposed to be looking out for Matthew, but as the months went by, he'd come more and more into himself and was less like that shell of a person he'd been when her father had happily exclaimed that his son was returned to him.

She hadn't known she'd had a brother until about seven months or so ago, but she also couldn't recall her life beyond the last year and a half. He explained that her memory issues were due to the life-threatening illness she'd had, and the experiments that had saved her life.

She didn't remember her life before waking up, before that moment she came to, her father patting her cheeks, demanding she open her eyes. She couldn't remember her life, and she relied on him to tell her everything. She hadn't believed him when he said he could shift into a fox. Not until he did it in front of her.

And then Matthew...

When he came back to them, their father had to keep him in a med pod. For a long time.

"He's healing," their father had said, never explaining that the young man in the liquid, sleeping peacefully, was her own brother.

When he woke up, Matthew nearly drowned in the pink goo that had been sustaining his body, and even when he was pulled out and dried off, his head lolled around, his eyes looking at everything and seeing nothing.

Rachel had to hand-feed him some mush she'd prepared from the garden so he wouldn't choke and then teach him how to speak and walk. Reading was next on the list. Something Matthew struggled with even to this day and hated to have rubbed in his face.

She knew he was embarrassed about it all. To be treated like a baby and have to be fed and cared for while he recovered, though Rachel never teased him about it.

"I'm sorry. You're right," she said quickly, shame filling her. "I'll stay away. I was just curious, I think. I don't know."

Matthew stuck his hands on her shoulders. "I won't let our father hurt you," he said, the softness in his voice making Rachel's throat close. "I promise."

"He wouldn't."

Matthew made a face like he didn't totally believe that but sighed and pulled back. "Come on. I'll take you to him. I think he wants us to go back to that place again tonight."

"The FUCN'A compound?"

Matthew made such a face that Rachel had to hold back a laugh.

"Are you sure you're not teasing me with that name?" he asked, scratching at the back of his head. "It sounds so..."

"Vulgar?" Rachel supplied gently.

Matthew frowned. "Is that bad? It sounds bad."

Rachel tried to think about what vulgar properly meant. She didn't exactly know, she realized. Sometimes she was also learning words. When she tried to remember classes or someone teaching her how to read, she couldn't. Her whole childhood was a blank.

"Yes, it can be bad. And... disgusting? I suppose." She didn't mind explaining things to him.

Matthew nodded, trusting her knowledge.

She smiled, putting her hand into his. "Let's go see our father."

Explaining herself to him would be another, more frightening, matter.

3

"Daddy's pissed off with you." Gerard waved his long, tentacle-like fingers in Rachel's face. Each shiny, slimy, wet-looking digit was complete with a hooked claw and suction cup.

Rachel cringed away. Her father's office door was closed, the lobby empty, illuminated by a lone flickering, sterile light. In the distance, she could hear the sound of dripping.

Matthew punched the man in the shoulder, and not in a friendly way, glaring hard. "Shut the fuck up, Gerard. No one asked you."

"Tough words." Gerard's beak shuddered. His oversized skull throbbed in time with his heartbeat. "You even know what *fuck* means, baby boy?"

Matthew's face turned bright red.

Rachel grabbed his shoulder, but he was stronger, pushing his way forward and shoving Gerard hard. The man made a splattering noise as he hit the wall, recovering quickly. Like he always did.

He surged forward, like lightning, his long, wiggly

fingers latching around Matthew's throat, pushing him backward.

Rachel shrieked when they both went down, the sounds of flesh smacking against the tile heavily. She thought she heard a cracking sound, but both men continued to fight.

With Gerard coming out on top. Matthew's face turned blue as he wheezed.

"Stop it! Stop it!" Rachel shoved at Gerard's back. He ignored her like she was nothing.

Rachel rushed for the office door and banged on it instead. "Daddy!"

Gerard wouldn't stop. Rachel pounded harder.

"Daddy, open the door!"

A heavy shriek sounded behind her. She looked, watching, horrified, as Gerard was lifted off the ground and nearly crushed into the nine-foot-high ceiling by the sheer size Matthew grew to.

His owl form was enormous in size, larger than a bear. And with unbelievable saber-toothed fangs as thick as her wrists. They looked more like white tusks growing out of his mouth.

In his oversized owl shape, Matthew was terrifying. Rachel's heart drummed against her ribs. Matthew was forced to duck his head, unable to stand at his full height as he stared down at Gerard.

Head tilting.

Like he was staring at a juicy worm. Or some fresh sushi —probably more fitting since Gerard was a sort of hybrid octopus shifter.

Blue rings glowed along Gerard's body. He smiled, though his lips quivered, sweat forming at his brow. "Yeah, try me, pretty boy."

"That's quite enough of that."

Rachel jumped. She hadn't heard the door open.

Bazyli Smith walked out, back straight and head held high. His suit was neatly pressed, as though he were preparing for a dinner party with the king of England.

His presence alone was powerful enough to soothe Matthew. The owl-beast still held the octopus-man but no longer looked as though he wanted to eat some seafood. His eyes focused on their father, feathers no longer bristling.

"That's right," Bazyli said, flicking his wrist at him. "Control your temper. We spoke about this."

Matthew folded in his wings, ducking his head, as though ashamed.

"Gerard attacked him," Rachel said.

"Yesh," Bobby slurred, appearing behind Bazyli. "It's never their fault, *ish* it?"

Rachel wondered why Bobby had been inside the office. Getting reprimanded? She could dream. Most likely he was filling her father in on her visit with John.

"Did you get scared, sweetheart?" Bobby stepped in closer, grabbing her by the arm, his mandibles clicking uncomfortably close to her face.

"No." She shoved Bobby away, angry with him, and angry with Matthew, who, even in his giant owl shape, hunched his shoulders.

Their father snapped his fingers up into Matthew's face. "Back into your human shape. Now."

Bazyli was skinny but tall. He was a fox shifter, nothing overly frightening, but there was just something very commanding about his voice. Something that made even Rachel want to shrink away from him when he was issuing directions.

Matthew blinked those big, owlish eyes of his, seemingly coming back into himself as he did as he was told.

His body changed back slower than he'd transformed, feathers merging and melting back into skin. Now, he seemed paler, almost smaller as their father approached him.

Matthew was naked, shoulders hunched, making him look smaller than Bazyli, even though they were the same height.

"You know better."

"I know, sir," Matthew said quietly.

"Prick," Gerard muttered, bumping his shoulder hard into Matthew's.

Bazyli snapped his finger at Gerard. "You, too!"

Gerard stood a little straighter, and Rachel was stupidly pleased that he got some of that guilty air around him, too. Even Matthew seemed to be fighting off a little smirk.

Rachel didn't like that her brother was standing there with nothing to wear, having shredded his clothes again.

"Daddy?" She cleared her throat, using the name he insisted she call him. "Daddy?"

Bazyli slowly angled his torso, glancing back at her, bushy brows lifting. Then he smiled. "Yes, sweetheart?"

Rachel swallowed. "Can I... Could I grab something for—"

"No."

She snapped her lips shut.

He turned his steely gaze back to Matthew. "You ruined another set of good clothes. You can walk around like that until you learn some control."

"Yes, sir." Matthew nodded, keeping his hands in front of himself. Which did almost nothing to spare his dignity.

"And *you*." Bazyli snarled at Gerard, who straightened instantly. "You remedial idiot, if you pick another fight like that again, you won't get your medicine, you understand?"

Gerard's big, glassy eyes widened even further. He nodded, a bubbly, airy noise coming from his lips. "Yes, sir."

Bazyli looked at Bobby and then back to Gerard. "The both of you, get the hell out of here. I need to have a word with my children."

"Yes, sir," Bobby scoffed, making sure to roll his eyes when Bazyli's back was to him.

Rachel looked at her brother then quietly entered the office. Matthew followed. He always did, closing the door behind him while their father sat down behind a big metal desk.

It was bright inside, the monitors serving as windows showing blue skies and sunshine, flickering slightly with age. The sounds of birds and trickling water came in through old speakers.

Rachel used to think there was a real-world on the other side of those monitors until she saw actual daylight for the first time.

Everything in her home seemed colder and darker after that, but aside from the grow room where she slept, Bazyli's office was the warmest and nicest room in the whole facility.

"Your heart is thudding, sweetheart," Bazyli said, putting his spectacles on. He adjusted them with one finger so they flashed in the fake sunlight. "Are you all right?"

"Yes," Rachel said quickly, sticking her hands between her knees. "I'm just cold."

"Hmm." Did he believe her?

Bazyli tended to be the suspicious sort, and his anger could be intense. He didn't always strike her, but whenever he did, it broke her heart a little.

Had Bobby informed him of her visit with John, or not?

He looked at her for one, two, three, four long seconds. Then he stood suddenly, walked to the thermostat on the wall, and adjusted the heat, increasing it by two degrees before returning to his seat.

"Better?"

Not that she could feel it yet, but she nodded.

"Now," he said, pulling some papers closer, "things are about to change around here. FUCN'A has been getting more... uptight, for lack of a better word."

The power flickered suddenly and went out. Rachel tensed. It took a moment for the emergency generators to whirl to life and another for the lights to come back on.

Bazyli had reached for the black filing cabinet next to him, steadying himself. He never liked it when the power went out. Rachel often wondered if he was secretly afraid of the dark. She'd never found out, though, as there were enough barrels of fuel to keep their generators running for weeks.

Not that they needed that much. Real power would come back shortly, and all that gas would work as their backup for years to come if rationed property.

Bazyli shook himself. "Anyway, I suspect we are running out of time."

"Are we in trouble?" Matthew asked.

"Not as of yet, though we will be, especially if they see *you*." His eyes flashed. He always issued dire-sounding warnings, especially aimed at Matthew, though never explained why.

"Why do they hate us so much?" Rachel wet her lips, feeling herself shiver and shake, despite the heat kicking on.

"Because we are not meant to exist, my sweet."

"That's not..." She stopped herself, biting her lip before she could say something as stupid and childish as *that's not fair*.

Of course it wasn't fair, and her father wouldn't appreciate her saying something so obvious and stupid.

"I know, my darling, but they don't like unnatural shifters. That anyone with the right equipment could attain their power is a threat."

"But you said we had to. I was sick, and they... did something to Matthew."

She still wasn't sure what that was. Bazyli hadn't given so many details, explaining that she wouldn't understand them. All she knew was that when Matthew showed up, he was a slobbering mess who couldn't speak or eat or stand without help.

The fact that he was as normal as he was now was, according to Bazyli, nothing short of a miracle.

She didn't want to contemplate what they'd done to him. Matthew clearly didn't either by the way his shoulders went stiff, so Rachel didn't delve deeper into that.

"They would leave Bobby to suffer as he is, despite having their own cures. They would have left you to die." She heard the edge in Bazyli's voice. She knew not to push him further. He didn't like to discuss this.

Rachel nodded. "Yes, Daddy, I know. I'm sorry."

"Hmm," was all he said then picked at a stack of rough-looking papers, some glued and taped together, and Rachel recognized that they were the shredded papers she'd collected from the FUCNA dumpsters on her last outing with Matthew.

"These papers are helpful, sweetheart. I'm very proud of you for obtaining them."

A rush of warmth and pride swelled in Rachel's chest.

"But this is all a dead end. You won't be needed to go to the surface again."

"But, why?" That warmth fizzled out like a dying

balloon. She didn't understand. "You just said I was helpful."

"Rachel…" Her father's tone was a warning.

She should let it go. She shouldn't argue, but she couldn't help it either. "I was doing good. Those papers—"

"Are personal notes written by the cadets of FUC. Not anything important. Those fools never just toss out anything useful to my research."

Rachel felt her eyes burn.

If she couldn't be useful, that meant she would be forever cooped up here. Underground.

She wanted to go outside.

"I can still help." Her voice sounded like a soft whine even to her own ears.

"No. The information I need is locked up in cabinets and protected in computer files that need passwords. Unless you've developed sudden lock-picking or hacking talents, then you're of no use."

Rachel's jaw dropped. Seriously? Her hands clenched and unclenched on her knees. It wasn't fair. There had to be something else she could still do. She could still handle herself. She knew how to stay out of trouble, to not be seen or caught.

With a heavy sigh, Bazyli rose up from his seat, walked around the desk, and pulled Rachel up. His arms wrapped around her, warm and solid. His thick fingers stroked through her hair softly.

The hug felt suffocating.

"I'm sorry, sweetheart," he said.

"I can be useful."

"You are," he said. "You can keep assisting me in the garden. The lilies are showing great promise, and Bobby needs them. Your work is important there, yes?"

She supposed that was true. Bobby never shut up about how he needed this plant or that to fix his shifter form. Not that she wanted to see what he looked like as a real spider. Would he be large and oversized, as big as Matthew's owl shape?

She shuddered at the thought, part of her not wanting to fix him at all if that's what he would turn into.

"There, now, all is better. See?" Bazyli pulled back from her. With his white hair pulled back from his face, he almost looked young, gentle, and sweet.

"Okay, I'll tend to the flowers." She reminded herself that important work was being done in the facility. Many people were counting on them. If they'd lost so many other staff, then she needed to see herself as an important member of the team—even if she wasn't allowed to leave.

"That's my girl." He stroked his thumbs across her cheeks. "Now you run along, stay out of trouble for me, yes? I have some things to discuss with your brother."

That good feeling Rachel had talked herself into fizzled. She left the office, glancing back one last time at Matthew just as Bobby pushed his way past her, the door closing behind him while they spoke of secret matters that she wasn't privy to.

She told herself to suck it up. She was not a child, and she would not act like one, even if she didn't like being on her own while not knowing what the others were doing.

At least the garden would keep her occupied.

Though it did give her plenty of time to wonder which day would be her last there before FUC agents showed up and arrested her for having shifting powers she wasn't supposed to.

The thoughts wouldn't leave. She couldn't find peace among the plants.

But she could think of one way she might be able to distract herself.

Rachel shook her head. She wasn't allowed. Bobby might not have told her father on her yet, but he might still. Wouldn't it be better to ask forgiveness for one indiscretion, than to be caught in a second occurrence?

Besides, there was no need to see John again, and it was dangerous to try.

Immature to go to him just because she was curious.

So she *wouldn't*.

She wouldn't...

4

It had been three days since John saw the woman with the red hair.

Two days since he'd seen *anyone*.

At least he wasn't on the table anymore. That was a bonus.

Some poor bastard with a wide forehead, bulging eyes, and tentacles for fingers had shown up and given him a few shots before unstrapping John from the table and tossing him into a cell.

A cell with bars easily escapable for a cobra.

Which was when John realized that he must have been shot up with something that prevented him from shifting.

No matter how much he tried, no matter how perfect his concentration was, it was as if there was a block in his mind and body.

At first, the realization gripped him with a cold terror. Mind-numbing fear that he'd forever lost the ability to shift. *After all I went through to get it!*

No. After a mind panic attack and some breathing exercises, he focused well enough to come to the conclusion that his shifter was still there. The cobra, powerful and strong, ready, coiled up, waiting to be set free.

It was just... not happening.

Which was weird because it felt like the loss of a limb he knew he still had. Like how he'd still known he had hands even if someone stuck oven mitts on them and secured them on with duct tape. He still had his hands, could still *feel* his fingers, but couldn't use them at all.

So, his cobra was still there. A small comfort, but he'd take any, considering the cold concrete around him and steel bars were his only company.

He had no bed. Was that because they didn't care to give their prisoners any luxuries, or was he a special case? Deprived of amenities in retaliation for the part he played in past experiments?

Or had they assumed he could rip up a cot and use the materials as weapons?

He definitely could have, so it was smart to not give him one.

Thankfully, there was a small sink and a toilet he could use. John didn't want to think about how he'd been using the bathroom while passed out on that table. He still had some pride left, so being able to clean himself up was a small comfort. Both the sink and toilet were made of metal and built half into the wall so he couldn't pull out any parts to use.

The place was old. This facility was not like the one his previous captor had been working out of. Not that *her* setup had been much better.

Here, the walls and ceiling dripped and moisture hung in the air, which meant he was either very close to the surface or there were a few floors above him that needed the plumbing seen to.

He wondered if he could remove the small tap at the sink to try digging at those wet cracks. If he could chip away little by little, he might be able to dig a hole and wiggle his way out.

Assuming he was near the surface.

And assuming no one found out what he was doing and tried to stop him.

And assuming he could turn into his snake again.

But it had been two days.

He had water, but he was starting to get worried and starting to feel nauseous from the lack of food. Maybe they'd dumped him in there and forgotten about him. Maybe no one was coming back for him and he'd wasted two days when he should have been trying to escape.

He moved to the bars. He could only count the weird scratches and odd shapes in the walls so many times before he was too bored even for that.

He started to bang his fist on the bars.

The echoing sound seemed to travel far, which felt empty and terrifying.

"Hello?" he yelled.

The empty cells around him, some with flickering yellow and blue lights, gave an almost horrible non-answer.

"Is anyone out there?"

He waited. Only the echoing drip of the water traveling through this terrible place could be heard.

Holy shit. What if they really did abandon this place? What if they'd been raided and no one had bothered to look for or find him?

He knew how often that could happen in places like this. He'd gone from place to place plenty of times before... with *her*.

Many facilities had been built, half-built, abandoned, or

were still in full working order, set up by the people that came long before *Mother*.

Mastermind for example. *Mother's* personal hero.

Mastermind had set up the whole structure for everything happening with the illegal underground labs, long before her whole shitshow came to an end.

Had Mr. White-Haired Fox Shifter taken off to another location? Had he been raided and arrested?

Either way, that pretty red-haired woman would be gone, and John would die alone.

No. He knew that FUC was more thorough than that. Maybe they were making their way through the facility and just hadn't gotten to the cell block yet.

John pounded harder on the bars. "*Hey!* Is anyone there?"

He looked back at the tap on the sink. Somehow, the idea that he could attempt to escape if he *was* well and truly alone wasn't the comforting thought it should have been. Instead, he was filled with dread.

If they left him here, without the ability to shift, and no FUC agents were coming...

They'd basically left him to die.

The hunger pains in his stomach were so, so much worse. He'd spent too long thinking there were other people around when he could have been digging his way out, searching for more weaknesses in the bars or walls while he'd still had some strength.

The water could turn off down here at any point, and if those lights went out and he was alone in the dark—

A loud, screeching noise yanked him out of the spiral he'd found himself sucked into. Like being thrown a life vest after drowning, he grabbed onto it and came up for air, real-

izing for the first time in days, he was in the presence of
another.

His thoughts came together, and he began to think
clearly as he laid eyes on the woman with the red hair. His
heart hammered, and the sweat that had formed on his
spine and the back of his neck suddenly felt cold and sticky.
Is she really here? Or have I begun to hallucinate?

If she really was there, then that meant he was not alone,
wasn't abandoned—an immense relief.

It also meant there was no possibility of escape—a
terrible disappointment.

He watched the woman walk in with a light step. She
had on the same clothes as the last time he saw her, that
ratty green dress that went to just below her knees, and now
he could also see that she wore black flat shoes that looked
like they'd come out of a trash bin.

Surely he'd hallucinate some better clothes for her,
wouldn't he?

"How long have you been in here?"

"Long enough to wonder if you're all checking to see how
long a snake shifter can go without food." He tried to hide
just how freaked out he'd been. "Where the hell is everyone?"

The woman glanced back to the door, as though
wondering just that.

"I... You're hungry?"

John pressed his hands to the bars of his cage, a little
embarrassed with himself for panicking, but still trying not
to let it show. "I've been alone in here for a few days, so,
yeah, some food would be great."

He didn't want her to suspect that just two seconds ago
he'd been in a whirlwind he couldn't escape from.

Or that she had been the one to yank his ass out of it.

That gave her entirely too much power, and she already had so much, considering he was in the cage... and she wasn't.

Her shoulders went tense. "Oh! I'm... I'm really sorry. I didn't realize—"

"You didn't realize people needed to eat?"

"Of course I know people need to eat. I just wasn't aware that you were in here not being fed." She sounded annoyed, but also confused. He almost felt sorry for her.

He stopped himself. Lowering his guard would just get him into more trouble.

"What would you like to eat?"

That threw him off. "Seriously?"

"I mean I can get you a sandwich and some coffee."

He lifted a brow at her, his gaze traveling up and down her body. He could only see her pale legs and the smooth curve of her collarbone from beneath that overly wide neck of her dress, that baggy thing, which, if not for an equally oversized belt, left practically everything to the imagination.

But she was definitely pretty.

And he was in a mood.

"If you want to talk about what I'm craving, you can come over here and I'll tell you."

She actually took two steps forward before stopping.

"No. I can't."

Annoyance flared inside him. "Why? Because your boyfriend, Matt, will have something to say about it?"

Disgust warped her pretty mouth and nose. "Matthew is my brother!"

Right. He'd assumed that already. It was nice to have the confirmation, though. Something ugly and green inside him settled down. "Oh, well, all the better for me then."

She frowned, clearly not understanding what he was

saying. Which sort of took the fun out of it. She couldn't be that obtuse, right?

"Come on over here. I'll tell you what I want."

She eyed him, suspicious. She was right to be.

"Tell me what you want to eat now, and I'll go and get it."

Fuck.

It would have been nice to grab her and search her pockets, if she even had any, for a potential key to this thing, but it seemed like that wasn't going to happen.

He needed strength if he was going to escape, and he needed food to get that strength, so he might as well take what was offered.

"What do you have again?"

"Uh, well, there's a few turkey sandwiches in the kitchen. Some pea soup left over. We have coffee, tea, and water. There's some apples, and there might be a few chip bags left."

He couldn't tell if she was offering him all this sarcastically or if he was actually going to get to eat it. His stomach constricted painfully, the nausea from a lack of food hit him hard. He couldn't bring himself to be too proud to make the request.

"Honestly, all of it sounds fine. I'm starving. I won't be picky," he said, adding, "Please."

He was willing to humble himself just a little if it meant getting fed.

At least to her. If it was Bobby, that ugly-looking spider motherfucker, then he might just be a bit more of an asshole for the sake of being a proud asshole.

A pretty woman offering him food, however... He could say the magic word for that.

Especially when she smiled at him like that. Softly. Not like she had something sinister planned.

"Wait here. I'll be back."

Right. Like he had a choice.

He felt that familiar panic rising up inside himself as she rushed off, back out the way she came.

She didn't shut the door behind her. Why would she think she had to? He was locked up safely behind bars. He wasn't going anywhere.

But that sense of loss, of emptiness, with the only sounds around him the distant echoes of singular drops of water from leaking pipes and the buzzing electricity of those dying lights around him, filled him with a sense of being almost buried alive. He started counting, fighting everything inside him to keep from yelling after her to hurry up and come back.

Christ, he might even take Bobby or that squid-looking guy over this insane sense of loneliness.

But she did come back, with an honest-to-goodness tray of food in her arms and an eager smile on her face.

As if she was getting ready to serve a friend or a guest and not... whatever the hell he was supposed to be while he was here.

"Okay, I brought you a little of everything that I could find," she said. "I think Gerard was supposed to feed you, but I don't know where he is, and he might've forgot."

John didn't take his eyes off that tray. "Gerard is the guy with the slug-looking fingers?"

He wiggled his own fingers, as if she needed the visual.

"Um, yes." Her eyes went wide, and a hand immediately flew to her mouth, as though she was trying not to laugh. "But that's really mean."

Now John could only stare at her. "I'm in a cage."

Her cheeks colored, the rosy tint hiding the many freckles she had. "Oh, right. Sorry."

As if she had anything to be sorry about.

He hated this. But he deserved it.

She stood another five feet or so away from the cage, as though unsure of what she was supposed to do now. "Uh, maybe I'll put this on the floor and slide it toward you."

Clever. She seemed innocent enough, and maybe she was, but at least she knew better than to let herself get within grabbing distance.

Because John absolutely would grab her if given the chance.

He would hate to hurt her or scare her. She seemed nice enough. He wasn't getting the sense that all this was an act, but then again, he wasn't exactly the best judge or that sort of thing either.

She got to her knees, setting the tray filled with food on the floor and slowly sliding it forward. The instant it was within reach, John grabbed for the first things his hands would touch.

The sandwich first and the wrapped-up honeybun.

She didn't yank the tray back. She let him keep taking from it.

There was a can of soda, the promised small bag of chips, and even some cookies and apple slices. The soda can was a mistake. He hoped she wouldn't ask for it back when he finished with it.

There was a Styrofoam bowl of pea soup, as promised. He had to be a little more careful with that so it wouldn't spill.

She still didn't remove the tray.

There was a small roll of bread, a few mini packs of butter, peanut butter, jam, and even, to his immense shock, a cutlery set.

It was the sort of thing that was tossed into takeout bags.

Wrapped in plastic with an extra dry napkin, and likely have one of those little wet napkins inside, he could see the plastic fork, spoon, and knife.

He grabbed it. Not trying to be too quick about it or too slow either. In her rush to be a good host, she'd probably stuck the thing onto the tray without thinking about it, without thinking that she shouldn't be giving their prisoner anything he might use to escape or harm his captors.

Just as she hadn't thought he could twist the aluminum soda can into a deadly weapon if he wanted. She was just trying to be helpful. Kind.

He wouldn't be cutting his way out of these bars with a little plastic knife or an aluminum can, but he could use it to defend himself, should Bobby, Gerard, Matthew, or that white-haired fox come back.

The woman pulled the tray back when there was nothing left on it, as though worried that was the thing he would use as a weapon. It was hard enough plastic. If he broke it, there would be some sharp edges, but he'd gotten what he wanted.

For now.

"Thanks for all this," he said, tucking the cutlery set away and looking at his sudden riches.

"You're welcome. I'm sorry no one was feeding you." The woman smiled back before her face turned concerned and she glanced back at the doorway. "I shouldn't be down here, though."

John immediately pulled the plastic wrap off the sandwich. "Why's that?"

"Because you're dangerous," she replied.

Which stopped him for a moment as he took the first bite. Then, he shrugged it off, continuing to chew the sandwich, which was a little stale, but glorious and delicious, before swallowing. "Yeah, that's true."

The woman looked at him, as though expecting him to elaborate. "What did you do? I heard you were an agent of FUC."

He tried not to laugh. A choked sound rushed out instead, shame warming his face. "No. Never was an agent. I was a cadet though. I was learning how to be an agent."

"Oh," she said, her eyes darting around, as though she were deep in thought.

It was interesting to watch while he opened and savored the honeybun. Christ, that was good.

"Are you not a real shifter either?"

"What?" He almost choked again, opening his Coke can so he could quickly drink.

"I'm not a real shifter." She spoke softly with a tinge of sadness in her voice. "I was sick. Something happened, but I can't remember much of it. My father had to turn me into a shifter so I could get the healing ability and survive."

Made sense. That was what *Mother* had been after, so this motivation wasn't shocking. He did wonder, though, why she was sharing the information with him… and how much more he could get out of her. "What sort of shifter are you?"

She grinned, her freckles practically glowing under the light. "A red panda."

He thought of what they looked like.

Tiny things. Like her.

"Sounds nice."

Definitely friendlier than a snake.

"Do you want to see?"

"N—"

She shifted immediately before he could tell her he had no interest.

It was quick. She vanished in the oversized green dress she was in, the whole thing falling to the ground, a small lump crawling around inside the clothes.

Then, out of the skirt end of things, her animal shape, a red panda, crawled out.

He stared. She stared back.

Then she sat back on her haunches and lifted an arm to wave at him.

Adorable. She would have no issues making friends among other shifters. It was always the cute ones, or the majestic ones, that were valued. The bunnies, the bears, the squirrels, and even the wolves and goddamn moose were preferred to cold-blooded reptiles.

He wanted to laugh. "Yeah, you're real cute."

The fluffy red panda in front of him froze and then rushed back up the skirt of her dress, shifting quickly into a human once again.

She looked a little embarrassed as she sat on the ground across from his pen.

John was impressed.

"Not many shifters can keep their clothes good shifting like that."

She pushed some red hair behind her ear, where it promptly popped back out of place. "I've had practice."

He nodded. He bet she did.

Unfortunately, that made his mind go to all sorts of places it shouldn't be going.

He had to get off that train of thought. He, instead, focused on how she'd reacted when suggesting he was a FUC agent. "So, why don't you trust FUC?"

She jumped a little, pulling her knees up, crossing them

at the ankles, though being very careful about keeping her green dress covering anything he might be able to see. "FUC agents don't like it when humans mess around with the natural order of things. They don't want normal people to have shifting powers."

He smiled miserably. "That what he told you?"

"Yes." She frowned, tilting her head slightly. "What else could it be?"

He opened the chip bag, his stomach already settled, feeling so much better than before. At least hunger-wise. As far as his feelings toward this woman, that was a whole other issue. He hated what she was saying and the way she sounded. He hated that he used to sound the same way.

"Look, FUC is a bunch of holier-than-thou, stick-up-their-asses pricks, but they are right about protecting the natural order of things."

"What do you mean?" The woman's frown deepened. "I would have died without this. And I *like* being a red panda now. It's a part of me."

Like his cobra was now a part of him, but that was not the point.

He shrugged. "Maybe they would have let you die. Maybe they wouldn't have. I don't know, but I used to think the same as you. That they just hated anyone else having access to the power they did." He popped a chip into his mouth, trying not to think about...*her*.

About Charlie. A woman he'd once cared about. A friend turned chinchilla after they'd signed up together. A cute and fluffy animal who'd once owned his heart, though he should have never been dumb enough to believe in love. He shook his head. It had taken a while, but he'd finally gotten over her.

"That makes no sense," red-haired girl said, popping him out of his thoughts.

"It's not that they hate that anyone can be a shifter," John explained. "I'm sure that's part of it, but what they really hate is when some evil cartoonish scientist with a god complex comes along and manipulates desperate, hopeless people into experimenting on themselves and fucking up their lives and bodies. That's what they hate. They hate the kidnapping, they hate the lying, they hate the torture, and they hate the ruined lives that come after the fact. That's what they *really* hate."

The woman shook her head, finally looking at John as though he were dangerous. Not just some houseguest for her to impress.

"No one was tricked here. Not me, not Matthew. Not even Bobby or Gerard. FUC threw them away. They weren't helping them when they needed it."

"Sure thing, sweetheart. Whatever you want to think about it."

Her kind and curious expression turned sour. She shot to her feet, her small hands clenched. "Don't call me that!"

"Oh, but you were so kind to give me all this food, baby."

Her cheeks reddened even further. "Don't call me that, either!"

He wasn't helping himself, he knew it, but her inability to see what was going on pissed him off. He'd been that naive once, following around a woman he called *Mother* and doing her bidding blindly. Standing by while she experimented on the willing—and not-so-willing.

He'd even assisted Mother by kidnapping a pregnant woman so Mother could steal her baby.

A baby John was relieved had been returned to the woman in question after only a few blood tests on the little tot. Something so, *so* much worse could have happened, yet he'd done enough, playing his part in it all to ensure he was still going to be seen as a monster for the rest of his days.

The scars on his face itched.

He had to do something to distract himself. He wanted to get a rise out of the woman in front of him. Because, why the fuck not? He was already a villain. Might as well play the part. Even if it drove her away.

He didn't deserve the company of a nice woman. He didn't deserve the food he was eating now.

He deserved to be alone. Distraught, going mad from loneliness.

"You know, since I already have you serving me with a smile, when you're feeling up for it, you could bring me some blankets and a pillow. Folded neatly if you could."

He swore he saw her whole body bristling. "Screw you."

Heat rushed through him. "Hell, if you want to, we can. I won't say no to you."

The woman's mouth opened and closed several times. She seemed at a loss for what to say.

As if he'd reached into her throat and plucked the words right out of her.

In the end, she said nothing. Holding the plastic tray to her chest as though it were a shield, she spun around on her heel and marched toward the door.

John watched her go.

A little triumphant.

A little sad.

She stopped and turned back to look at him. He stared back. And was stunned when she reached to the side and flicked off all the lights before exiting his cell.

Leaving him in perfect darkness as the heavy metal door screeched shut and clicked with a heavy lock.

He blinked several times, his eyes never adjusting.

Well, fuck.

Apparently, that innocent-looking little redhead had some bite after all.

And he hadn't gotten her name yet, either.

Double fuck.

5
———

Matthew hated slinking around town like he was some sort of criminal.

He hated digging around through trash cans. He hated spraying cameras he spotted with black paint, and he hated having to hide. He especially hated having to do any of these things with Bobby, the miserable prick.

If he had to deal with the wet sound of Bobby's breathing again and again from his mouth, the hairs and mandibles shuddering with each breath he took, in and out, in and out, again and again, he might lose his mind. But at least Bobby was shockingly quick at the keyboard, which was something.

He cursed a lot under his breath, the computer screen making a couple of buzzing noises before he finally got what he wanted.

Matthew still didn't fully understand computers. Or the Internet.

Rachel's knowledge was also fairly limited, but she had told him that everything left a trace. There were cameras on computers, and anything posted to the Internet was likely to stay there forever.

He shuddered to think of such a horrible thing, but right now, it was their way of trying to find information about the FUC agent's experiments while steering clear of the actual FUCN'A facility.

There was an office where a couple of doctors worked who were familiar with their practices. The nameplate on the desk read Diane. Matthew was pleased that he could read that name without much effort. His practice was paying off.

It was dark. In the building and outside of it. Everyone in the office had been home for hours. They should have time, but Matthew was antsy. He didn't like being here.

He stood to the side of Bobby as the man stared at the screen, growling a couple of times under his breath about something or other. Matthew never got right in front of the computer, however, worried one of those cameras that Rachel always told him about might be there.

"Motherfucker," Bobby slurred. "Thosh dirty, rotten, *evil*...

"What? What are you looking at?" Matthew angled his head just enough to see the screen. On it, there was a photo of a couple of people.

They had to be other shifters. One of them, a woman, had something sticking out of her forehead, heavily bandaged.

Like a horn.

There were a couple of people in white doctor's coats standing next to her, and a young man with the brightest, happiest smile on his face Matthew had ever seen.

Bright, golden eyes, too.

There was a man in plain clothes as well. Glasses on his

face, his arm around the shoulders of a slender woman with long, brunette hair, with a toddler in her arms.

The chubby kid wore blue overalls with a fist stuck in his mouth and what looked like a stuffed Harry Potter owl dangling from his other hand.

Aside from the young man with the golden eyes, they drew his attention the most. He was pretty sure that was the woman whose child John helped to kidnap.

Matthew didn't approve of what FUC was doing, but what John and his previous boss had done was pretty horrible. Taking a baby from a mother... Well, that seemed wrong on so many levels.

Matthew searched for something wrong with the photo, anything else that would explain what had triggered Bobby's anger. He saw nothing strange. It looked like a photo of friends or colleagues, but it was possible there was something obvious happening here he wasn't picking up on.

Yet Bobby still seethed. He practically vibrated in his chair. He pounded his fist on the desk, three times, hard enough that the monitor jumped and the image on the screen crackled.

"Stop that! You're going to break it!" Matthew might not know much about computers, but he knew they were fragile things.

"Shut up!" Bobby snapped back, his eyes flashing. He looked like a spider ready to bite. "You don't know shit!"

Much as he hated Bobby, Matthew had never seen the man so furious.

Matthew wanted to clock him, but instead, he spoke in a level voice, hoping Bobby would get a grip on himself. "I know that Father will be pissed if you break this before getting the important information off it for him."

Bobby snorted. "Right, it's important all right."

He pressed some buttons and then growled. "Bitch hash everything pashcoded."

His words were more slurred than usual. He didn't usually talk like that unless he was really mad. For the most part, and with enough effort, Bobby could typically get his words out sounding normal.

Matthew assumed that whatever Bobby was looking at must have something to do with the people who hurt him, who refused to work on a cure for him despite the obvious problems his face would cause with going out into the world.

Such a shame. Everyone in the photo looked so... normal.

But that was part of the problem. They were at peace with their shifting abilities. They weren't stuck in some horrible space in-between like Bobby and Gerald were.

Bobby tried inputting some more passwords, getting blocked at every turn before finally giving up.

"Who the hell puts a password on their printer?" he growled, pulling out the burner phone Bazyli had given to him and taking pictures of the screen itself.

"Don't know," Matthew replied, pretending he understood what was and was not normal when it came to computer security.

Everything Bobby did on that keyboard, including how quickly his fingers moved, seemed like magic.

The guy was an asshole, but his knowledge of computers was impressive, and it was clear to Matthew just why Bazyli kept Bobby around, despite his poor attitude about everything.

"That's all we'll get," he said. "Unless we want to take the whole damn tower."

What tower? What was he talking about?

"You mean this?"

"That's the *screen* you idiot," Bobby snarled, hitting some more keys and shutting down the screen Matthew had been pointing at.

He shot up from his seat and approached some file cabinets.

"You're sho shtupid," he slurred, pulling out some tools to pick at the lock. "If it weren't for your shtrength, there'd be no need for you."

"Sorry? Say that again, I couldn't understand what you said with all the saliva in your mouth."

Bobby spun around shockingly quick, pinning him with a menacing stare, the hairs and mandibles around his mouth shuddering.

Matthew didn't back down. "Are you picking the lock, or aren't you?"

Bobby sneered at him then went back to work.

He got the cabinet open in short order, his work so neat and clean there would be no sign that anything other than a key had been used at all.

Once again Matthew was stuck having to give Bobby the credit for being good at what he did. While Matthew, as per usual, was stuck keeping watch in case someone showed up.

Bobby pulled out file after file, taking multiple photos of everything. It took a while to get through one cabinet, but Matthew had to admit this was infinitely more efficient than what he and Rachel had been doing digging around in dumpsters.

Bobby was oddly quiet for a few, blissful minutes, not even coming up with something sarcastic to say. It left Matthew the chance to snoop around the office, searching for something Rachel might like, something small that would not be missed.

He found a table in the waiting area that had some print-offs of coloring pages, along with some crayons and colored pencils. He took some of them.

Then he located the lost and found, which had a thin pair of gloves and a scarf inside. Rachel had been saying how cold home was becoming. He figured no one would miss those, either.

"You're picking up bad habits from that little trash panda," Bobby said, snapping more photos.

"Don't call her that." Matthew abandoned the lost and found, his pockets stuffed.

"Whatever." Bobby shrugged. Matthew thought he was done speaking, but all of a sudden, he shared something unexpected. "Those people you saw in that photo. The FUCN'A folks? Well, that guy they were all happy around was TJ."

Matthew had heard the name before but couldn't recall why it was important. "You didn't get along?"

"He was like me." Bobby pointed to his face. The fact that his words were less slurred now meant he was calm, at least. No less cruel, though. "Face more fucked up than mine. Teeth like long needles. He bit himself all the time, mouth always bleeding and drooling, eyes like a fucking google-eyed fish."

"Oh." Matthew didn't understand.

"They fixed him." Bobby shook his head, closing the cabinet and locking it again.

Matthew didn't know what to say. He'd been taught that FUC was the enemy, yet in this instance, it seemed like FUC had *helped* someone.

"Yeah, well, TJ was always a little ass-kisser." Bobby shook his head, staring at the cabinet.

He looked like he might punch it.

"They *cured* him," Bobby continued. "They took their sweet fucking time... made all the excuses in the world why they couldn't get on with it..."

"Are you sure he didn't just finally learn to fix it on his own?" Matthew asked. "If that's possible, you could learn to control the shift as well."

"Huh." Bobby blinked. He looked at Matthew with an odd expression on his face, which was already saying something. "You're not so stupid, are you?"

Matthew immediately regretted trying to make him feel better. "Are you done here? We should go."

"Yeah, nothing but a bunch of patient shit anyway. Stuff for tummy aches or kids with food allergies." Bobby wiggled his phone. "All here if *Daddy* wants it."

Matthew nodded. He was fine with getting the hell out of there anyway.

Except, Bobby got that faraway look in his eye.

"What?" Matthew asked.

Bobby shook his head. "Nothing. Let's go."

It wasn't nothing. Matthew could tell. Bobby was making plans for something. His plans were usually on the reckless side of things.

"If you're thinking of—"

"Let's go," Bobby snarled, marching past him, banging their shoulders together.

Matthew had no choice but to follow him.

He did another once-over of the office.

Aside from the items he'd taken, which he doubted anyone would notice, there was no trace anyone had ever been here. He and Bobby had worn gloves, and the only true sign of a break-in would be the paint on the cameras, but there was nothing to be done about that.

Matthew had quickly learned it was impossible to leave

zero trace of his presence. They could only be as quiet and quick as possible in their missions.

So, to make it appear as though they had been searching for something other than information, he and Bobby made sure to bust open a few cabinets in the back room and take as many bottles of medication as they could stuff into their pockets.

Painkillers, vitamins, sleep medications, the works.

Bobby even pocketed a few needles, which Matthew hoped were for re-stocking their labs and not some other plot Bobby might have.

He both hoped and dreaded the thought, that those could be for their prisoner and no one else.

6

Rachel immediately regretted turning the lights out on the man being held in the cell block. She knew what it felt like to be in the dark, with nothing for her eyes to adjust to.

It was eerie. And scary, especially with the other sounds of the facility dripping or creaking or rumbling around her.

But she couldn't bring herself to go back and turn them on again. Not after all he'd said.

What rankled the most was that he hated the agents of FUC, but he defended them, too. She didn't understand that.

It left her a lot to think about while she pruned the dying leaves from the lilies in the garden.

Why was there a part of her that believed him when he spoke about the reasons why FUC did what they did?

Even so, she knew with certainty that FUC wouldn't have allowed her father to save her. They prohibited experimentation like the kind that had saved her life.

Rachel had been sick. She knew that. She could barely remember anything about her own life except for the tiny snippets that came to her when she dreamed. She saw her father sometimes, and a woman she thought might be her mother, but Bazyli never liked to talk about that.

She saw herself playing on the swings, strong hands pushing her higher and higher. Then riding in the back of a car, Bazyli spinning around, angry, telling her to stop kicking his seat.

She couldn't remember Matthew at all, but that wasn't surprising with how little memory she actually had. She couldn't recall what her mother looked like, where she went to school, or who her friends were, so that just made sense.

But she remembered that she had been sick. So had her mother.

Her father had saved her by turning her into a shifter. Apparently, he hadn't been able to save her mother. But at least he'd saved Matthew.

And that was the big difference between what her father was doing and what the man in the cell accused. She and Matthew had not been taken. They had not been experimented on. Bobby and Gerald had both come to work for her father willingly.

Rachel let her finger gently slide down one of the soft petals of the lily she'd pruned.

Her father was good. He was upset before his wife died because he couldn't protect his children without people judging him for it. He kept them all safe, he loved Rachel and Matthew, and he was trying to grow these beautiful flowers because they could help more people.

That was all.

Later that night, Matthew came back with gifts for her, taking her mind off of the terrible conversation she'd had with the snake shifter. She loved her new orange scarf, and the gloves would help her stay warm.

Then there were the pencil crayons and pages Matthew handed to her. Shyly. He wasn't exactly a practiced thief.

"You like them?" he asked when she took them, staring at the pretty pictures.

"I love them! Thank you!" She threw her arms around him, happy when he hugged her back. "I'd have been happy with nothing but you coming back safe, you know?"

It seemed important to tell him that.

He squeezed her tight. "I know."

"Did you find anything else?" She meant for their father.

He knew. "I'm not sure. It was Bobby who spent most of his time on the computer and then in the cabinet, taking pictures of files. There was... something. It might not be a big deal."

Now she was really curious.

Rachel grabbed his hand. "Tell me about it, and look at how well the lilies are doing. They might be useful soon to help Bobby and Gerard, and anyone else having trouble shifting."

"Yeah," Matthew said, not sounding nearly as enthusiastic as she did. "FUC might already have something to help with that."

She didn't understand. "What do you mean? They don't believe in this kind of medicine."

"I know, but Bobby saw someone..." Matthew shook his head, apparently deciding he didn't want to speak anymore on the subject. "Never mind. Where's Gerard?"

Rachel blinked. "I thought he was out with you."

"What? No."

They looked at each other. Was Gerard out on an errand for their father, or was he off on another one of his hairbrained schemes?

"He hasn't been feeding the man downstairs." The words slipped from her mouth.

"How do you know that?"

Crap.

"I just went to check on him."

"Rachel." Matthew sighed. "Did you give him anything?"

"Yeah, I did," she huffed. "I wasn't going to let him starve, no matter how much everyone tries to convince me that he's bad."

"I mean, did you leave anything with him? Anything he could use as a weapon?"

"I took the tray back so he couldn't break it. There was only garbage left."

"I'll check in on him myself." Matthew didn't seem pleased. His mouth twisted into a fine line.

She tried to think of anything on his lunch tray that could be used to hurt someone. And was suddenly reminded of when she'd seen Bobby, in one of his less-than-stellar moments, crush a root beer can before he started to peel at the metal.

He'd used the sharp bits to start cutting away at the thick hairs growing in and around his mouth.

She'd been disgusted watching him and had to look away from him even though he'd been doing it at the lunch table. Maybe that was why she didn't remember until now that she'd given him a soda can.

She told Matthew, who groaned. "Rachel."

"I'm sorry!"

"I need to take it from him. Was there anything else you gave to him?"

"I..." She tried to think. If anything could be a weapon, then didn't that mean everything she'd given him could be used to hurt people? Even the plastic wrap around the sandwich?

She tried to list off everything she'd handed over. Napkins, sandwich, bread roll... The soda can was, so far, the most important.

"Okay. I'll take it from him."

"What if he tries to hurt you with it?"

"Then I'll hurt him."

Rachel's heart seized to hear her brother speak so casually about doing someone harm.

He seemed to take that for something else. "I won't tell our father. Don't worry. But I will ask Gerard why he's not doing his chores."

"I want to go with you. When you ask for it back."

"What? No, you're staying here."

That rare anger she felt for her brother rose up inside herself. She hated it when he tried to get too protective of her. And though she didn't know that man downstairs, she hated the thought of him getting hurt.

It didn't matter what sort of weapon he had. He would never be able to fight off Matthew if he really wished to take it from him. Not with how big Matthew's saber-toothed owl could get.

"I'm going with you."

"Rachel—"

"Unless you want to lock me up, you can't stop me." To prove it, she marched past her brother, back straight, hands clenched, already on her way down the hall.

Matthew sighed, following her. "I could, you know," he said, his voice gentle. "I could grab you, put you into the garden, and lock you inside. You wouldn't be able to stop me."

She kept moving, knowing she was being unfair. That

she was taking advantage of him.

"I know, but you won't."

He wouldn't because she was the only person he could talk to down here. Gerard and Bobby weren't exactly friendly, and she was his only sister. He would want to stay on her good side.

And she... Well, she knew he would forgive her for this.

So long as she wasn't hurt.

"I'm just going to ask him for the can back," she said. "I was nice to him earlier. Maybe he'll give it to be nice back."

"That's not how keeping a prisoner works," Matthew growled, the both of them taking the stairs.

It was no longer dark down there when they arrived, suggesting someone had come along and turned the lights back on.

Maybe Gerard?

Either way, Rachel was secretly pleased to see it nice and bright down here.

Matthew immediately pushed himself in front of Rachel, storming over to the only cage with a person inside it.

She had to rush to keep up with his long legs.

"You've got something."

Rachel came to the front of the cage, seeing the man inside, leaning against the wall, tossing something into the air. Catching and tossing, again and again.

"I don't have much of anything," he said, his whole body going suddenly stiff as he smiled at Rachel. "Did you bring me a pillow?"

Guilt ate away at her. "Uh, no, but I will bring you one if you want."

"That would be great," he said, tossing his ball into the air again.

A ball, which turned out to be made up of the plastic wrap that had been around his sandwich.

More guilt attacked her, burning at her skin. He really didn't have much to do down here. It made all her complaints about not having many personal possessions seem trivial. She had a wonderful collection of items, things to keep her occupied, clothes, and even chores, compared to him down here.

"I'll bring you a nice pillow and blanket, but you have to give back the soda can."

He stopped when the wadded-up ball of plastic wrap landed in his hand again.

He looked at her, then at Matthew, and smiled, a short, barely-there laugh escaping him. "Figures. Should've known you'd only visit me for that."

She didn't understand what he meant by that, but to both of their shock, he moved to the toilet, reached inside, and pulled the can out.

It was still in one piece. It hadn't been crushed or ripped into sharp bits that could cut someone.

Rachel still grimaced at the sight of it. "You kept it in the toilet?"

He stared at her, deadpanning, "Where else was I going to hide it?"

Fair enough.

Still gross though.

Matthew didn't seem to care as he reached through the bars, holding out his hand. "Give it to me, John. Now."

There was a clear threat in Matthew's voice, a tone even Rachel didn't hear too often.

John, if that was his real name, simply looked at him. "I'd rather give it to her," he said. "Here, I'll even make it nice and clean before handing it over."

He ran the water in his tiny sink, put the can in, and soaped it up, along with his hands.

Rachel still wasn't sure she wanted to touch it.

"You can give it to me."

"I can give it to her, or you can come in here and get it yourself, tough guy," John said, not even bothering to look back at him.

"I can take it," Rachel said.

She stepped forward. She was determined to do this. To show she wasn't afraid of him.

John glanced back at her. His smile was... soft. As though he was relieved.

"Rachel, don't," Matthew said.

Rachel stuck her hand between the bars, holding it out for him. "It's okay. If he does anything, you're here."

She didn't take her eyes off John. She wasn't scared of him. The way he looked at her, though, still sent a shiver through her spine. Not unpleasant, though, like the way Bobby sometimes looked at her.

"I fed you. I'd like the can back, please," she said.

"Then you'll give me something to actually sleep on?"

"Yes," she promised.

She meant it.

John tapped his fingers against the side of his leg.

Matthew was a bundle of energy she could feel vibrating in the air.

"Okay," John said and slowly, so very slowly, occasionally glancing toward Matthew, walked up to her.

Matthew growled.

Rachel didn't move.

The air felt strangely charged. Her breath caught when John came close enough to touch. Then he did.

His palm was rough, but warm against the back of her

hand, holding it in place, as if he needed to, before settling the wet, clean can into her palm.

She curled her fingers around it, her heart hammering, her throat dry.

"Thank you."

He nodded. "You're welcome."

Then, he reached out and snatched her by the front of her dress, yanking her closer to the bars as fast as any cobra was expected to be.

Before she even knew what was happening, his arms were around her, holding her by the waist and the back of her head.

And then...

His mouth was on hers.

There was a strange buzzing in her ears and tingling on her lips that was both hot and cold at the same time.

She heard Matthew shouting, but it sounded so far away.

But then she processed that John had let her go because Matthew was punching him, through the bars at the side of his head, immediately breaking contact between them.

Rachel fell away, clutching the can to her chest, that ringing in her ears still very much there as she fell to her knees.

"Rachel? Rachel!" Matthew's hands were on her shoulders. "Are you okay? Say something."

She shook her head. She couldn't say anything. Nothing would come out of her mouth after that.

He was a cobra. He'd just put his mouth on her. He'd kissed her.

He'd *poisoned* her.

"I... I want..." She couldn't get the words out. She struggled so hard, but they wouldn't come right away. "Upstairs."

She needed the infirmary. She needed to get something for poison. What was needed for a poisoned kiss? She had no idea.

"I'll kill you!" Matthew roared, rounding on the bars as if he was planning on walking right through them and attacking the man inside.

John barely looked at him. He was still on his ass, looking up at Matthew.

Then he glanced at Rachel.

She couldn't read his expression. He didn't seem happy about what he'd done.

It didn't matter. She had to get out of here.

"Matthew!"

Matthew looked at her, his face a bright shade of red, though his eyes immediately were calm as he was back at her side.

"Help me get out of here."

God, she was so stupid. Matthew hadn't wanted her down there, and she'd insisted on going, so of course something bad had to happen.

She had no one to blame but herself. Everyone had warned her. Bobby certainly had. Matthew told her to stay away. Yet she'd pushed the limits and was now reaping the rewards.

Matthew pulled her up from the floor and helped her walk out of the room.

She'd dropped the can, but that was fine. It was far enough away from the bars that John wouldn't be able to reach it.

When she looked back at him, she saw he wasn't looking at the soda can. He was staring back at her until he was well out of sight.

7

Rachel's mouth tingled, and her whole body vibrated the entire way to the infirmary.

Matthew said some things, but she couldn't understand a word that came out of his mouth, even when he was practically yelling in her face as she sat on a metal table.

All she could focus on was the poison. And struggling to breathe.

Oh my God, I'm gonna die. He killed me. I don't want to die. Please don't...

"Rachel!"

She blinked, snapping her head back, processing the state that Matthew was in. He'd become panicked, with feathers popping out of his forearms while he gripped her shoulders.

Like he was struggling to hold himself in check.

"Breathe. Take deep breaths. I need you here with me," he said, though he almost could have been talking to himself as well.

"Am I going to die?"

John was poison. She'd been kissed by a snake shifter, and this was all her fault. She'd been warned not to touch him, to not go near him, but she kept pushing her luck, and now...and now...

"You're going to be fine. I promise. I just need... I need..."

Matthew looked around, struggling.

Because he didn't know what she needed any more than she did.

While they still had an infirmary, it wasn't staffed by anyone and wasn't well-stocked either. What medicine could she take? What antidote was there for cobra-shifter venom? If any existed, did they even have it in their crumbling facility?

"Maybe... maybe lie back," Matthew said, pushing her back on the table. "Lie down and keep calm. Keep breathing slow."

"Right. A quick heart makes venom pulse through faster." She could vaguely recall learning that information somewhere. Probably in one of the many animal books she'd paged through.

Rachel lay back, staring up at the ceiling while Matthew opened drawers and cabinets, making so much noise as he searched for anything useful. Not that he would. She was sure he wouldn't.

Her lips still tingled. She felt lightheaded.

Her first kiss and it just might kill her.

Well, if John never got fed again, that would be entirely his own fault then, wouldn't it?

"I don't know what to do." Matthew came back into her line of sight, looking very wild and frantic. "I'm sorry, Rachel, but I have to go get Dad."

Rachel nodded, feeling a strange sense of calm wash

over her. She'd dreaded her father finding out that she'd visited John, but now, her father was her only hope.

He could save her. Just as he had when she'd been sick.

Matthew was there one minute, and then he was gone. Rachel was alone. And cold. She pulled the scarf Matthew had given her a little tighter around herself. Would her father notice it and yell about it before or after he saved her life?

It didn't matter. She was even more glad to have the scarf. It was something to hold, something to comfort her while she died.

Except, the slow, tired slide into nothingness never came.

After a moment, her mouth stopped tingling. Rachel could no longer feel the heat of John's mouth on her lips or the press of his hands on her lower back.

Those things went away. Her lightheadedness vanished, and she was still very much alive and well when Matthew did not return after several minutes.

Rachel sat up. She looked down at her hands, as though there could be some mistake.

John's very touch was supposed to be poison, and he'd had his hands all over her. He'd touched the back of her head, his warm lips against her own. That heated, tingling sensation briefly returned, but it felt more like something she would have dreamed.

Rachel took a deep breath.

Then another.

And then another.

The feeling she expected from a poisoning did not come. She did not feel nauseous. She didn't feel *bad*.

The heat, that lightheaded sensation, and the burning

from his hand on the small of her back had all been there. A symptom of something intoxicating and wrong.

But she no longer seemed about to die.

Which was good news, especially when Matthew returned, his eyes wild with fright and shining with desperate tears.

He seemed shocked to see her sitting up. "Rachel, you should lie down."

He tried to push her back, but she held her position.

"I'm all right."

Matthew stopped, looking very torn between desperate hope and disbelief.

He wet his lips. "Lie back and rest for me anyway. I'll get you some water to drink."

She did as he asked but only because he seemed wilder, more jittery than herself.

"I can't find Dad," he admitted, coming back to her with a glass of lukewarm water from the tap. "Drink this. Maybe it will dilute the poison?"

Rachel drank but only because of how thirsty she was. Matthew watched her like he expected her to burst into flames.

She handed back the glass. "I think I'm all right," she finally said.

Matthew's chin trembled. "Are you sure?"

Rachel did one last internal check of herself. No sickness. No more heat. Not even that pleasant tingling against her mouth.

Though there was still the ghostly feeling of John's hands on her body. Not at all an unpleasant feeling, she was shocked to discover.

"I think his poison missed," she said.

"Is that possible?" Matthew asked, more desperate hope in his voice.

Rachel nodded. "I don't feel sick."

And it was the only explanation, though even she knew it couldn't make sense.

How could his poison have missed when his mouth and hands were so very directly on her?

Matthew, always the excellent brother, didn't seem to want to take any chances with that.

"I'm going to put you into bed anyway. I'll bring you more water. I want you to rest. For the rest of your life."

It was so ridiculous that Rachel couldn't help but laugh at it. "I can't be in bed forever."

She had chores to do. And their father would wonder what was going on with her if she didn't get up.

Matthew shook his head, grabbing her shoulders and yanking her to his chest. He held her tight. "Just promise you'll be okay?"

Rachel was struck dumb by the smallness of his voice. She lifted her arms, gently setting them around his massive shoulders.

"I'm all right," she said again. There's nothing else she could say. Nothing that could truly convince him other than the strength in her voice.

She really was all right.

And yet...

John's kiss *had* done something. She couldn't quite put her finger on just what that was. The word *infection* didn't seem right. It was too sinister for whatever this was.

Even now, however, she felt it growing inside her.

Not life-threatening, but consuming all the same.

MATTHEW CARRIED Rachel to her bed in the garden, despite her protests that she could, in fact, walk.

He didn't care. He wouldn't risk that she lose her energy and something would happen along the way.

Aside from their father, she was all he had. And she was his best friend.

He couldn't believe that disgusting snake put his hands on her. Matthew was going to break his knees.

He tucked Rachel in and brought her another glass of water, along with some crackers to snack on in case she got hungry.

Rachel insisted she was not tired, but he wasn't having it.

"Promise me you'll stay here," he pleaded.

"Don't hurt him." She grabbed his wrist with a shocking strength before he could turn away. "It was my fault."

Red-hot fire shot up inside his belly and chest. He pulled away from her hand. "That was not your fault."

"I gave him the food, and we got the can back. I should have known—"

"He's the devil, Rachel." There was another word he wanted to use, something infinitely more hateful and venomous, but he didn't have the vocabulary, so he couldn't find it.

Devil would have to do.

"Those sorts of people take advantage of others. He's already done bad things before. Of course he would want to hurt you."

Rachel swallowed. He couldn't name the expression on her face.

Matthew wished he was smarter. He wished he knew how to help her, how to make this better other than putting her to bed and promising her everything would be okay.

He needed to ask their father for the chance to study some more, because if all he had was his hands, if all he was good for was threatening to break people if they tried hurting his sister... Well, when someone like John came along and actually hurt her, no amount of pain inflicted would take away the damage already done to her.

"I'm going to talk to him. That's all."

Rachel didn't seem fully convinced, but there was nothing she could do. She let him go.

An hour later, Matthew stood outside the room with the many cages. His heart thudded and his gloved knuckles were bloody after his time with John.

He yanked them off and tossed them away, and his hands ached. Yet, he was not satisfied.

The man hadn't even tried fighting back, which, Matthew now realized, was what he'd wanted.

No matter. There was nothing that could be done until he found out where his father had gone.

Where *had* his father gone? He hadn't seen him since he and Bobby had handed over the photos. He'd tried to follow along with the conversation, but he only understood bits and pieces of what his father and Bobby discussed.

FUC had cured someone. They were hypocrites. They were experimenting on shifters. They were using their medicines on their favorite subjects, making their lives easier while Bobby suffered.

Matthew thought of the young man in the photo. Thought of the way he smiled as he stood next to the woman with the bandaged horn.

A horn that, apparently, could help shifters who had trouble controlling their shifts. Those who were stuck in monstrous hybrid forms.

Matthew rubbed his burning, swollen knuckles. Perhaps a little of John's poison had made it through the gloves he'd worn. He examined the pair, looking for holes and finding none. Just blood.

Everything is in the blood. Something his father had said before, and the words ringing in his head made him think again about that man with the smile.

If he'd been cured... did he have the magic in his blood? Did he have exactly what his father was trying to create with all those useless flowers?

Matthew started to wonder... could he help his father by finding the man and bringing him back here for his father to study? The FUCN'A facility wasn't very far away, and if he was like others Matthew knew, like Gerard, Bobby, or even himself, then he would likely be out on his own from time to time. Enjoying the new freedom that came with having his face cured of the mess that had been made of it.

Matthew needed a shower. Needed a moment to think before he acted.

Also needed a chance to wash off any blood droplets or spit that had likely made it onto his clothes and perhaps his skin. He didn't want to suffer any of John's poison.

Though, thankfully, with Rachel recovering, it was likely that John's touch might not be so venomous after all.

Or poisonous. Because there was apparently some sort of difference. Something else he wasn't quite sure of.

Matthew washed up, did one last check on Rachel, then left a note for Bazyli that he would be off hunting for fresh meat to bring back to the facility.

It wasn't entirely a lie, and Matthew doubted he would be so lucky as to find what he wanted on the first night, but he had an idea of where to start. Bobby always spoke of going to the bars again when, and if, he should ever become normal, and there was one local bar in the tiny mountain town.

He had some cash on him, and he could think of nowhere else a new shifter would wish to be after having his face repaired.

So Matthew would start at The Hub.

8

Despite not being tired at all, being tucked in so warm and snug after such an eventful day had put Rachel to sleep.

When she dreamed, she dreamed of him.

John.

They were both standing by the bars of his cage. He had his arms around her, his face close enough that she could make out the slight bump in the middle of his nose.

Had it been broken before? She opened her mouth to ask, but nothing came out.

The ease with which he touched her felt unlike anything she'd ever before experienced in the whole of her life.

She wanted more.

But she had so many questions.

He touched her forehead. He smelled of something... horrible.

"What's that?" she asked, recoiling but unable to leave, as she was trapped by something behind her.

It startled her awake. Rachel snapped her eyes open to see Matthew was there, wiping her forehead with a damp cloth, as though she were on her death bed.

She pushed him back when she realized the strange and awful smell was coming from *him.*

"You stink," she groaned. "I was having a nice dream."

He smiled, though there was nothing happy in it. "Sorry. Are you feeling better?"

She thought about it. "Yes. I think I was just... tired."

"He won't touch you again."

She snapped her gaze at him. Matthew sat on the side of her bed, a guilty expression on his face, his shoulders hunched, wearing clothing he only ever wore when he left the facility.

"Where did you go?" she asked, a little sad that he'd left without her.

And a little regretful that she had not been able to use that time to go back and ask John why he'd kissed her. Had he been trying to poison her? Or... was there another reason?

"Just searching for more information." Matthew shrugged.

She didn't detect a lie, which was strange because it did feel as though he was hiding something.

"Didn't find what I wanted, though."

"You smell strange." She leaned in for a sniff. Something smokey, and something sweet.

The scent of other people.

Alarm blared inside her. "Matthew, what did you—"

"I went out. That's all." He shot to his feet. "I'm going to shower it all off anyway."

She couldn't blame him for his carelessness. Not after what happened to her yesterday.

In fact, she was a little jealous. "Where did you go?"

"To a bar."

A bar! That was so exciting. "What was it like?"

Matthew seemed to think about it. "Not like what I saw in the TV shows you put on for me. There was a little music, some TVs turned on to sports channels. Mostly food. No fighting. There was a trivia game. I got invited to play."

"Really?"

He nodded. "I declined, which was good because I didn't know any of the answers."

"Oh." She was a little sad about that. Even if he didn't know the answers, she would have liked him to have tried.

"So what did you do?"

He sighed. "I ordered some nachos. Watched the people. Watched the TV. I learned people take soccer very seriously in Europe. There were lots of fires happening."

"Oh. Their team lost?"

"I think their team won," he said, scratching the back of his head. "But I'm not too sure."

She grinned.

"And the smoke smell?"

His cheeks actually colored a little. "I, uh, was invited outside to try. I don't think I like cigarettes. I had one and puked."

Rachel burst out laughing.

Matthew shoved her shoulder. "Don't tell Dad."

"I won't." She would never. They weren't supposed to be out and seen among people. Not without good reason.

Matthew deserved a night to feel normal, and she hoped he had a good time.

Though she was still sad that he hadn't taken her with him. She would have liked to go, to be around normal people. That was impossible, though. For so many reasons.

She wasn't allowed out, but even if she managed it, she couldn't blend in. Her clothes weren't fit to be seen in public. Matthew had different changes of clothes that allowed him to get away with people seeing him from time to time. He could keep his hood over his head so no one could catch a glimpse of his face. His jacket was a little too tight for his wide shoulders, but he could still pass for normal.

Rachel liked her dress, and she was grateful for it, but she wasn't stupid. She'd seen enough pictures of other women to know that she would stand out wearing what she did. A thin, green dress that was too old, too big, and might make people think she had nowhere to live wouldn't exactly allow her to blend in.

In any setting.

At least she was smart enough to know she shouldn't try it. But just as she shouldn't have been visiting John, Matthew should also stay out of danger. "Don't be tempted to go back," she warned.

"I'm glad you're all right," Matthew said. "That's all I care about."

She left her bed. "I want to brush my teeth, and you need to change your clothes."

She stopped on her way to the sink, looking at him. He stood with a near-guilty expression on his face, his hands clasped behind his back.

She smiled. "I'm fine. Thank you for taking such good care of me."

He nodded. "Don't go to see John. When I find Dad, I'll talk to him about how Gerard has been neglecting his chores."

Rachel opened her mouth to argue then immediately swallowed down anything she could have said.

She wanted to see John. She wanted to ask why he did what he did.

And why he chose not to poison her with his kiss.

The way Matthew stared at her, his eyes pleading...
What could she do?

"I promise. I won't."

He looked so relieved.

Rachel hated to lie to him.

———

HER CHANCE TO see John came sooner than Rachel
expected.

She spent the day caring for the lilies, watering them,
checking their soil, adding more food, which they needed,
and clipping off excess leaves and imperfect petals for the
study.

Later that night, with his outside clothes freshly washed
and his hair neatly combed, Matthew announced he was
going hunting.

"Hunting?"

"The meat locker is getting a little dry," he said. "And I
got in touch with Dad. He gave his permission."

He was going hunting... wearing that? With his hair
looking like that? No, he was going back to that bar. She
knew he was lying, but she didn't want to accuse him. She
didn't want to make him feel bad for wanting to be normal.

"So where is Dad?" she asked.

"Out with Gerard, apparently." Matthew had a black
backpack over his shoulder. Probably so he could keep his
clothes in it after he shifted and flew back to town. "They're
pillaging some of the old compounds that FUC shut down
for anything useful. Not all of them were buried in cement."

Rachel shivered. She thought of FUC finding this place,
taking her and Matthew away. Or worse, pouring cement on
everything while they were still down here.

"You won't be alone. Bobby will be back soon. He'll take over John's feeding, too. So you won't have anything to worry about."

Rachel didn't like that idea much either. Bobby seemed about as trustworthy as Gerard. Crueler, too.

"Why are we keeping him again?"

"What?"

"John. Why does Dad want him here?"

She'd asked the question before and gotten non-answers. Been told they were doing tests on him. But now she had more information on John. She knew he'd betrayed both the Furry United Coalition, as well as the mission her father's people worked toward, but she didn't understand why he was being kept there still.

"I don't know, I never really asked," Matthew said. "He's a shifter like us, a human turned. Maybe his blood will help Bobby and Gerard."

Rachel doubted that. Her own blood, and Matthew's, had been taken plenty enough times that, if anything was there, she was sure their father would have found it by now.

"Anyway, I'll be back. Please stay away from him."

Rachel nodded, wishing him well, and she waited exactly ten minutes after he left, ensuring he was gone before she made her way to the kitchen and then downstairs.

The door seemed more imposing than ever before.

Rachel thought that burning, tingling sensation she'd felt in her mouth when John had kissed her was long gone, but standing here, getting ready to go inside, it came back with a vengeance.

Her heart raced. His hand was suddenly sliding around the small of her back and pulling her close.

She had to take a deep breath.

That was yesterday. He wasn't touching her now, and he wouldn't ever again. She would see to that.

Rachel took a deep breath, her fingers trembling slightly as she touched the door, leaning forward to peer through the small glass window.

She didn't see him, or anyone. She wouldn't until she got to the very end of the room.

She reached for the cold metal of the bolt that kept the door securely locked. She unbolted the lock and opened the door. The metal shrieked loudly, as it always did.

She shivered, pulling her new scarf tighter around her throat.

Why did it always have to be so cold down here?

She walked slowly toward John's cage, the inside becoming visible, but she didn't spot John until she was standing almost right in front, very far out of arm's reach.

John sat on the floor in his still-empty cell, his head down, his arms on his knees.

"I brought you another sandwich," she said, her voice more bitter than she'd expected. "And a juice box. With no straw."

She tossed both in his direction before taking a few extra steps back.

He didn't look nearly so imposing as yesterday, but there was a strange sense of danger in his silence.

She waited a moment.

He said nothing. He barely moved.

Rachel took a breath. "I wanted to ask you something."

His shoulders began to shake, as though he were laughing. "Like what, sweetheart?"

She pressed her lips together. She didn't have much time, and she didn't want to waste what little she had on correcting him.

"Are you surprised to see me alive?" she asked. "Did you try to poison me, and it failed? Or did you... well... was that kiss not intended to poison me?"

Even now, she wasn't so sure that was the case. Not when her lips buzzed and burned, as though all these hours hadn't passed at all.

She could still feel the warmth of his breath ghosting across her face and neck.

"Poison you?" He looked up, and his face...

She gasped.

He seemed confused by her words, but his face shocked her. His entire face was red, black, and blue. Swollen and cut up, much more than it had been when he'd first arrived with injuries from an animal attack.

She wondered what had happened, and when. Though he hadn't looked like that when she'd seen him yesterday, the wounds still looked old. Somewhat healed. On him, a shifter, he looked as though the worst of the swelling had already gone down. On a human, they might be a few weeks along in healing.

It was not a stretch to know Matthew had done this. Possibly right before he'd gone to the bar.

John pushed himself to his feet. "Why are you talking about poison?"

"Matthew hurt you?"

He blinked, touching the side of his face, wincing, as though he'd forgotten there was something amiss there. "Right, well. All's fair when I kissed his sister in front of him, right?"

Rachel wasn't so sure. John was in a cage, and Matthew was much bigger than him.

It didn't seem like a fair fight.

"I'll talk to him. He shouldn't have done that."

John stepped up to the bars, putting his arms up against them, leaning forward.

Rachel took another step back.

"I'm in a cage, in the ground, and no one knows or cares where the fuck I am or if I live or die. What's it matter to you if your big brother wants to rough me up a little?" He actually smiled. "It means you've got someone looking out for you. It's a good thing, to be honest."

"Is it?"

He rolled his eyes. "Of course is it. I know you know what I'm talking about."

He glanced down at the food at his feet. He didn't reach down for the food, however.

He kept looking at her. "Thanks," he said.

"You're welcome." Rachel straightened her shoulders, the need to defend her brother, even just a little, surging forward. "If he did that to you, it might have had something to do with his fear that you'd poisoned me."

"Why would you think I poisoned you?"

She blinked. "You're... you're a cobra, aren't you?"

"Yes?" he said, very slowly, a brow over his black eye lifting. "And I currently cannot shift because of what your Daddy did to me."

She didn't like how he said the word, *Daddy*. As if he was mocking her for it. She clenched her hands in front of her. "Even so, I was told you're poisonous to touch."

He barked a laugh. "And you believed them."

She didn't know what to say. Rachel was struck speechless as her brain worked that over.

"God, you're really naive, aren't you?"

"No!"

"Yes, you are." He kept right on smiling at her, as if he found the whole thing to be funny.

"How exactly is it such a stretch to go from 'this guy can turn into a snake' to 'this guy's skin is poisonous,' huh?" She glared at him. "Look at Bobby, with spider mandibles? I have no reason to not think that someone has a toxin coming out of their pores."

"Point taken." He shrugged. "But you should probably ask yourself, what else is your asshole *Daddy* lying to you about?"

"Nothing," Rachel quickly replied, mostly because it had been Bobby who'd told her John was poisonous, not her father. "Are you going to tell me next that it's not true that you hurt people?"

The smile faded from his lips, and the scars running down his lips and cheeks seemed more prominent at that moment. "Yeah, I guess you got me there."

Her heart wouldn't stop racing. She couldn't stop feeling his mouth on hers. His hands on her waist. She couldn't stop wondering what that would feel like if it happened again.

"So why did you do it?" she asked. "Why did you kiss me, if not to poison me?"

"Because you were there." He shrugged, leaned down, grabbing the offered food. "And I haven't kissed a woman in a long time."

Something inside her deflated. Rachel wasn't sure what his explanation would be, but she hadn't expected that. Hadn't expected an admission that she was just an opportunity. That it hadn't even been personal.

He opened the juice box with his fingernail, taking a drink before seeing the look on her face. "What?"

"Nothing." Rachel shook her head, pulling her scarf up a little higher around her cheeks.

"No, not nothing." Whatever it was he saw on her, it had him interested. He leaned up against the bars again, that smile reaching all the way into his eyes. "You *liked* it when I kissed you, didn't you?"

A miserable heat entered her cheeks.

She *had*.

"It was my first kiss." Rachel absolutely should *not* have said that. She knew her mistake the instant it was out of her mouth.

She couldn't face John. It was too embarrassing. She turned and rushed out of there before he could humiliate her or tease her for it, slamming the door shut behind her, locking it, leaning against it.

That hammering was back in her chest. Full force.

Stupid. She was so stupid. Why did she say that? Why?

Rachel covered her face with her hands. That burning sensation swept all over her body. She couldn't seem to get a grip on herself. She couldn't take in a proper breath.

Maybe whatever he'd infected her with wasn't really poison, but he'd corrupted her all the same, and she had to stay away from him.

She had to get out of the facility.

Rachel wasn't brave enough to go into town, but she was an adult, and she wasn't going to be cooped up in here any longer.

She needed fresh air.

Rachel was going outside, and she was going to enjoy herself in her red panda shape.

9

———

Matthew wasn't sure what he was thinking, returning to the Hub.

Doing something he knew his father would be furious about.

Risking being caught by someone from FUCN'A.

Not to mention, he was going to run out of cash.

Money was already a luxury item, but cash in and of itself was especially rare. Sometimes his father would give him some cash so he could pay the few delivery guys they hired to bring in food or supplies, but mostly his money supply came from finding and taking any bills or coins he found when out and about.

And that wasn't much.

But he hadn't spotted any of the people from the photograph on his previous visit, and he wanted another chance at it. Felt like he *had* to find that smiling man. He was the key to something. Fixing Bobby and Gerard? Helping his father make a breakthrough?

When he arrived, he tried ordering a beer, but unlike the

previous night, this bartender asked him for ID. Something he did not have.

The guy glared at him, sizing Matthew up while Matthew insisted he was over twenty-one.

"I'm twenty-five," he said. "I was here last night. I had my ID, and I got served."

A lie, but he doubted the other guy who worked here would admit to serving someone without being carded.

"Sorry, no ID, no serve." The guy behind the bar didn't look happy, but at least he didn't kick Matthew out.

That was something, though it meant he had to order a soda to go with his nachos. He still tipped the bartender, because he knew that was something he was supposed to do.

Though it left him with even less money than before.

He took a seat in the back, somewhere he could watch the patrons. There was another trivia night happening. There were many couples. A lot of smiling faces, and a few, overly loud jokes that got a few tables banging.

It was interesting to watch.

This was not a move or TV show. These were real people he was looking at. Real people with real lives who probably had jobs. Some of these people might even work for FUC.

His sense of smell in this place was a little dodgy, thanks to the sheer number of people—especially shifters—and the food and booze in the air.

He started on his food.

God, it was so good. There were no nachos with messy cheese back home. He'd have to find a way to get it on the food order that his father made every few months.

He could imagine how much Rachel would like these, too.

He almost wished he could bring her here. This place

seemed safe enough, despite the FUCN'A facility being right up the road.

A waitress with bouncy hair and wide hips came along to ask him how he was doing. Her tag said Brenda, and her scent was distinctly shifter, though he couldn't tell what type. He smiled at her and got a free refill for his soda.

"You waiting on some friends?" Brenda asked when she returned with his freshened drink.

"No, just passing through." He shook his head.

"Well, I hope you enjoy yourself," she said, her eyes suddenly flashing.

Matthew tensed, glancing around.

"Don't worry. It's nothing." Brenda slid into the booth across from him and lowered her voice to a conspiratorial tone.

"Wha-what do you mean?" he stammered, realizing he was in a situation his father would be very angry about.

"You're tryna hide." She leaned in close. "Honey, only a criminal eats with his arms around his food and his hood up."

He swallowed. A steely, mechanical hand gripped his heart and squeezed tight.

"It's okay." She chuckled softly. "You've got much too innocent a face to be in trouble with the law. Whatever you've got going on is none of my business, but I have a feeling you're a shifter looking for somewhere to kick back and relax. Just like the rest of us." She gestured to the rest of the bar.

For some reason, her words made him relax. He let out a sigh. "Sorry, I've not been around a lot of other shifters," he admitted.

"It's okay! Just try to relax if you want to blend in. Otherwise, you're going to have some FUC agents noticing you and asking questions. Those nosey bastards are always hoping to catch the scent of a case."

"FUC agents." He lingered over the word. "You get a lot of them coming in here?"

He'd started to doubt that he was going to find the TJ person Bobby growled about here. And even if he did come to this bar, what were the chances he would be here at the same time Matthew was?

She nodded. "Don't you know their cadet training facility is nearby?"

"It's a training facility? I heard it was some experimental place." Not the truth, but he wanted to see her reaction.

"No way. FUC doesn't *do* experiments." She looked at him like he was speaking nonsense. "They take down those who are. You ever hear of a woman called Mastermind?"

He had. His father's work carried on what the iconic scientist had started.

Even so, he let the woman chat on.

She spoke of a few things Matthew knew to be true, that there were people out there, humans, who became shifters. Some chose to out of desperation or illness, but others were changed due to other circumstances.

Those other circumstances being kidnappings. Forced experimentation on people with little to no family. People who wouldn't be missed. And it all started because some tiny woman had a hatred for the sort of shifter she could become. So she'd wanted to change that.

"They were taking little kids and everything. Sick. FUC put a stop to that, luckily," Brenda said, shivering.

Matthew didn't like this conversation. Clearly, Brenda only had FUC's side of the story.

Even so, he couldn't discount everything she said.

Rachel always said that when people lied, there was a little truth to what they said.

So, how much of what Brenda was saying was the truth? What if she wasn't lying at all?

Or worse, what if she was and didn't know it?

Was this why his father was in hiding? Because the people of this town thought he was the bad guy?

What if they're right? The thought sent a chill through his body.

"You all right, hon?" Brenda asked.

"What happens to the people who are changed, but not for the better?" he asked, wanting to hear this woman's take on Bobby's and Gerard's situations. "Like if you get trapped as... part animal and part human?"

"Oh, FUC has been working on that. I don't know how, but apparently, they helped one fish woman already. Had scales all over her body that aren't there anymore, and this other guy, maybe about your age, whose face was affected."

"Affected how?"

She shrugged. "I've never seen what he looked like before, but he said he had these long teeth that stretched his lips and cheeks, sometimes cutting himself. The poor thing. It sounded awful, but you wouldn't know it to look at him now."

Matthew's throat went dry as well. She was talking about TJ, the man Bobby hated. "How do you know all this?"

"He told me." She blinked, looking at Matthew like it should be obvious before she turned in her seat and pointed across the room. "That's him right there."

How had Matthew missed him walking in? Perhaps it was just being in a situation with so many new scents and sounds. Or maybe it was because his tasks always involved locations that lacked interaction with people. Either way,

Brenda pointed to the very guy Matthew never thought he would actually see.

TJ's eyes were bright and lit up as he surveyed the bar. He wore a blue scarf around his neck, which he promptly took off as the doors closed behind him.

An act that messed up his perfect hair just a little, making it appear windswept.

He looked nothing like his photo.

He looked younger. More at ease and content with the world.

"Hey, TJ!" Brenda called, catching his attention. "C'mere. There's someone I want you to meet."

10

John waited for the woman with the red hair to come back.

She didn't.

At least she hadn't left him in the dark again. A small win. He supposed he would take it.

He ate his sandwich, drank his juice, and made sure his plastic knife was still hidden safely in the crack he'd carved in the wall.

Well, not carved. The constant dripping water and damp air had helped to crumble the wall just enough for him to pick at it, pulling away small rocks and pieces, until he had a place thin enough for him to put his only method of defense, should he need it.

Neither Bobby nor Gerard had come back to inject him with anything for a few days. Would his shifter be reachable soon?

He doubted the naive, pretty redhead had been putting anything in his meals.

Another small win.

So he spent the night alone, again, eyes closed, thinking about her.

About how soft her mouth had felt against his. About the slender curve of her waist and the generous mound of her ass against her hand.

About the fact that she'd said he was *her first kiss.* She deserved better than to have been manhandled by him. He took a chance, indulged in a kiss from her, without thought of what it might have meant to her. Without thinking that she thought her first kiss had *poisoned* her.

Fuck. He was trying to focus on shifting.

But he couldn't help himself. John's thoughts constantly went back to her. How she'd felt. How she'd tasted.

He really couldn't blame her brother for beating the hell out of him. John would have if someone had laid into his sister like that in front of him. It was probably for the best that John had no sisters. Or any family.

Charlie had been his only family, and even she was gone.

But it didn't ache as deeply as it once had. One kiss with the red-haired woman and he was already moving on.

So much for his loyalty to Charlie, but she was happy now. With someone else. Probably forgot John existed and didn't know or care about where he was or what was happening to him.

He tried shoving thoughts of the redhead from his mind. Kept attempting to focus and reach out to the cobra side of his mind, the part of him that was closed off but still very much there and alive.

Everything inside him, even with his legs crossed and his eyes closed, screamed *no.*

Unable to reach his cobra, his thoughts immediately bounced back to the woman.

Despite everything, he feared for her. He sensed that she

had no clue what was going on down in this place, and that ignorance was going to put her in danger.

John didn't know if anyone here—other than maybe her brother—actually gave a shit about her. The massive aching on John's face was proof enough of Matthew's dedication.

He felt a sudden change in his fingers.

John glanced down, noting the soft scales that formed along his hands, his two middle fingers slowly fusing together as his body tried to accommodate the shift he desperately wanted to give in to.

He smiled. The relief washing over him was a shock. He almost couldn't breathe for a few brief seconds.

But his relief was immediately extinguished when he heard the banging of a door outside the cell block.

John stopped the shift. Though it had taken some time for him to change his hands even that small amount, it took nothing at all to form back into human.

He heard the fox shifter's voice.

"Rachel, there you are. You weren't supposed to be outside. What did I tell you?" It was the fox shifter who spoke. He did not sound pleased.

"Nothing happened." It was the redheaded woman who replied.

So her name is Rachel, John thought. *A beautiful name for a beautiful woman.*

"I collected some herbs," Rachel added.

The sudden sound of flesh smacking against flesh made John jump.

Did that motherfucker just *hit* her?

He rushed to the bars as if he could fit through them in his current form. Of course he couldn't see anything. They were too far away.

"You are to never be outside without my permission again," the fox said. "Is that understood?"

There was a brief hesitation. "Yes, sir."

She spoke so softly that John almost couldn't hear it.

Was she scared? Was she angry? He didn't know, because John didn't hear anything else.

They were suddenly gone.

Though he did hear the infuriating sound of Bobby, hooting and hollering down the hall.

"Little girl thought it would be a good idea to—"

"Keep silent, you ugly arachnid!" The fox's voice boomed throughout the whole facility. John would be shocked if the birds on the surface hadn't heard that.

Even John gave a shudder.

His hands hurt. He looked at them and realized he was gripping the bars tight enough that his knuckles turned white. He could barely feel his fingers.

With a grunt, he forced himself to release the bars and step back.

He was pent up. A heat built up inside him that he needed to get out. He wanted to run. He wanted to fight.

He wanted to make someone bleed.

Preferably that goddamn fox for putting his hands on that sweet redhead... Rachel.

John envisioned himself as something useful. A shifter type strong enough to rip the metal bars away from the wall, to free himself. He wished he wasn't just some small cobra.

He wished he could be something like an anaconda. Huge, like some other shifters could be. Something impressive enough that Rachel would believe him if he tried to tell her that this place was all kinds of fucked up.

But there was nothing he could do.

He was not an anaconda. His animal shape was a

normal size for the species, and just because he'd failed to save Charlie didn't make it any less pathetic that he was fantasizing about saving Rachel.

She'd be disgusted with him if she knew his full story. Be horrified and never want to feed him again.

———

THE NEXT DAY Bobby came to visit him, bringing along Gerard, the shifter with the bulbous eyes and tentacles for fingers.

They had food with them.

A tray with a single sandwich on it. Two slices of white bread and a single piece of meat, along with a bottle of water. Hardly the generous offerings Rachel had brought for him previously.

"You gonna make this difficult, or are you going to eat it so we can leave?"

"There something in it to knock me out?" He knew the answer before Bobby smiled with those creepy, hairy mandibles of his.

Gerard looked irritated to even be there, but John didn't care about his problems, and he was a little hungry.

Whatever. He was tired of this shit, and it wouldn't be the first time he was knocked out and put onto a table.

He was so done with this bullshit.

John scarfed down the sandwich, staring right at Bobby while he downed the water bottle in one go.

"Whoa, brave one, aren't you?"

"Fuck you," John replied, belching for good measure. No point in being polite about it. Especially when his vision had already started to swim.

Drugs are quick.

He barely managed to catch himself on his knees when he went down.

The door to his cage opened, and he could distantly feel hands on him, dragging him out of his cage before everything went dark.

WHEN JOHN WOKE UP, he was back on the table, this time with something sticking out of his arm.

Weirdly enough, John was warmer and more comfortable than he'd felt in a long time. Except for his pounding headache.

And in the room with him, not his beautiful Rachel... but her smarmy-looking silver-haired fox of a father.

"What are you doing?" he tried asking, but his words came out only slurred.

"I'm looking." The fox barely glanced up from his papers on the clipboard.

"For what?"

The man sighed heavily, as though John were being a nuisance. He probably was, all things considered.

"C'mon." John tried to smile, but he figured there was a good chance it came off looking a little drunk and loopy. "I've been a good prisoner so far, haven't I? Barely made trouble for you at all. You can tell me why you're killing me."

"I can hardly kill you." The fox shifter snorted, which looked weird, coming from him. "I need your tissues and blood."

"If that's all you wanted, you could've asked." John made an attempt to move his arms, but they are definitely still strapped down. "Wouldn't be the first time I let someone experiment on me."

"Yes, so I've seen." The fox turned his back to John, looking through what might be a microscope. Hard to tell. Everything was so blurry.

John frowned. God, his vision was swimming. Was that a glass cylinder tank off in the corner? Filled with a pink liquid... and something else he couldn't make out.

Another tank next to it, this one about the size of a medium fish tank, started making an uncomfortable gurgling noise.

"Why am I alive?" John asked again.

"I just told you." The fox glanced back at him and sighed. "I need you alive because your blood and tissues are useful to my research. I would like to understand why your transformation was such a success, while Gerard, Bobby, and so many others were less than successful."

That doesn't sound so bad. That even sounds helpful.

He'd tried to be helpful with *Mother.* Only to learn that she didn't care what happened to those she experimented on in her quest to fix her own shifter form.

Wait.

"Is there something wrong with Rachel?"

That was usually why people signed up for this life. If not that, then a desperate need to escape something else. It was why he and Charlie had done it. They'd only had each other. No money, no prospects, and it could get her away from her father.

John was so lost in that swirl of thoughts that it felt like he blinked and, suddenly, the fox shifter was right in his face.

"How do you know her name?" His eyes blazed with fury, his hand gripping John's jaw.

"Bobby told me," John said, grinning as he took the

chance to nail it to the spider. "Likes to talk about her ass when he thinks no one listens."

"I will deal with him." The fox jerked back, disgust flashing across his normally stoic expression.

Interesting. The guy might slap his daughter for back-talking, but it was good to know he didn't want anyone speaking sexually about her.

So he *did* care.

That tank made another horrible, bubbling sound.

"Is she all right?" John asked, fighting against the need to sleep in the warm room.

"None of your concern." He returned to John's side with gloved hands, a small glass bottle, and a needle. "You speak too much for my liking."

He jammed the needle into John's arm. He didn't even feel it.

"If you're trying to help her," he said, the ghost of Rachel's face hazy in front of him, "I can help you. You don't gotta do all this on your own. I was mother's right-hand man. I have a lot of... knowledge..."

The shifter stared back at him as John faded. He couldn't read the expression on the fox's face because everything was suddenly swirling so badly that he struggled to keep from throwing up.

Rachel's face stayed in front of him, fading further and further away until he saw only red hair and green eyes.

SOMETHING COLD TOUCHED John's lips.

He slumped forward, blinking to try to get his vision back.

"Open your mouth," Rachel instructed.

"What?"

The spoon that entered his mouth held food. Some sort of chicken stew.

God, it was good.

"You've been here a while," she said.

Her face came into view. Her sweet, beautiful face. He frowned when he saw the slight red splotch on her cheek.

Was he imagining that? Or was that from where her father had struck her?

John swallowed and sat up straight then was shocked he could move at all. He looked at Rachel. "What's happening?"

Rachel grinned at him. "Bazyli decided you don't have to be in the cage anymore."

"Bazyli?"

"My father," she answered. "He said you both talked. You can walk around now."

"I can walk around now? Anywhere I want?" Holy shit.

No. Wait. That was too good to be true.

Rachel made an uncomfortable face.

"Not anywhere, asshole." Bobby's voice slurred.

John snapped his attention to the side, seeing the man standing there, arms crossed over his chest, making the seams of his T-shirt scream for mercy.

Bobby looked pissed. His eye was also looking a little swollen, one of his mandibles bent, as though someone had punched him.

John's face still hurt from when Matthew had decked him. It was either Matthew or Bazyli, the fox shifter. Didn't matter. John was happy either way.

"You have to have someone with you, for now." Rachel smiled at him. There was a light in her eyes that called to John.

Her happiness to see him out of a cage seemed genuine.

And that made something soft and warm light up inside him. She'd certainly seemed to have warmed up to him since the last time they'd seen each other. Maybe she'd gotten over her humiliation from admitting he was her first kiss.

"He said you volunteered to help us," Rachel said in a voice that sounded to him like hopeful.

"I did," John confirmed. Deciding to test his new freedom, he tried swinging his legs off the table.

And was immediately hit with a gripping, intense pain he felt all over his body. He screamed and damn near fell off the table as he lost control of his limbs.

The agony held him tight and didn't let go for an eternity. When it finally did, he was drenched in a cold sweat, gripping the side of the table he'd been lying on.

"Are you okay?" Rachel was on her knees in front of him, hands out, as though debating touching him.

"What... what the *fuck* was that?" John gasped.

"You try running or fighting, and you get another one of thosh," Bobby slurred.

John looked past Rachel to see that in Bobby's fingers was a small remote with a single button on it. Even if his face wasn't so fucked up, the smile in his eyes was more than obvious.

John reached up, his hands easily finding the collar around his neck that the remote was connected to.

Rachel took a breath, suddenly shooting to her feet and spinning on Bobby. "You didn't have to do that! What's your problem?"

"Keeping you safe, prinshesh," Bobby snapped back. He actually looked offended she would ask.

"I won't run." John shot to his feet, glad that Bobby didn't hit the button again.

John wished Bobby wasn't in the room, for so many reasons. One being he wanted to talk to Rachel about their last visit. About how he'd suggested to her that her father was lying to her, yet it seemed she hadn't told Bazyli about John's suspicions.

Well, it didn't matter. He could help Rachel, whether it was by helping her see this wasn't the place for her or by helping Bazyli come up with a potion or serum to cure whatever ailed the pretty redhead.

"Do you want more food?" Rachel pointed to the bowl of stew she'd been feeding him.

He'd forgotten about it. She'd placed it on a little side table. She probably stuck it there right when he got shocked.

He wasn't hungry, though. John had no idea how long he'd been strapped down for, and though it would be so easy to get lost in those big green eyes, he really had to piss.

"Where's the bathroom around here?"

"Oh!" Rachel looked suddenly embarrassed, as if she had any reason to be. "There's one right over there. This way."

"I'll take him," Bobby growled, pushing Rachel out of the way.

She glared at the back of Bobby's head.

John sneered at Bobby.

Bobby growled right back.

"Just go," Bobby snapped, shoving his shoulder. "Don't make me give you another one." He held up the remote.

This was going to be a problem.

If John didn't have to go so badly, he might have shoved back. He was lucky he hadn't pissed himself in front of Rachel when he got shocked the first time.

Whatever. If this was a test, then until he could get out of here and take Rachel with him, he needed to tread lightly.

Bobby showed him to the nearest bathroom.

John went in quickly, locking the door as fast as he could just as Bobby tried following him inside.

John had to be fast. Just because he didn't want Bobby following him in here to prove whatever he had to prove didn't mean he was fine with leaving Rachel out there with him.

God, it was a relief to use a normal toilet, though.

Could he still get back into his cell? He needed to find out fast so he could grab the plastic knife.

His chances of grabbing another weapon at some point were better with this new freedom, but there was no point in leaving it there to be found.

He quickly looked himself over in the mirror.

Pale didn't even begin to describe it. How much blood did that fox shifter take? There was really no need for the collar. He doubted he would be much of a physical threat to anyone.

Even to Rachel. No wonder the doctor was letting him walk around.

He tried pulling at the collar. It was strapped on good. Made of a thick leather material with a metal clip.

He might be able to cut it off with the right tools, though using any sort of blade to saw at the thick material around his neck didn't seem too appealing.

Or safe.

John needed to make plans later. He washed his hands and rushed back out before Bobby could try breaking in.

Bobby stood close to Rachel, his gaze angry. His fists clenched while he towered over her. To Rachel's credit, she gave back as good as she got. Her shoulders were straight and her spine stiff. Like a mountain facing down the wind, unmoving and uncaring of the storm.

Was this really someone who needed saving? She didn't look weak. She didn't look sick.

But it didn't matter. As long as it was possible that she needed his blood to help her, he was going to try and do it anyway.

He couldn't fail someone else. Not after he'd failed Charlie. Thank God she'd had someone else more capable to pick up the slack.

"All right. I'm done," John announced. "What does Bazyli want me to do?"

"You're to stay out of the fucking way." Bobby's shoulders remained tight enough that if John tapped them, they might shatter.

"Sounds vague."

"He wants to see you in his office," Rachel said, seeming to be speaking about Bazyli. Rachel turned her back on Bobby and faced John.

"All right, I'm ready." John took a breath.

The three of them left the room. He wasn't sure if it was a medical room or a lab. He didn't know what to think of it. He'd been in the labs of too many evil scientists, getting poked and pricked and prodded. They were all starting to look the same.

They walked through the windowless corridor, John thinking that this was no place for anyone. Underground.

Especially not a place for Rachel.

"When you have downtime, you can come into the garden with me," Rachel said as they walked. "There are lots of little chores and tasks that need to be done."

It sounded like she was actually offering. She even

seemed a little shy. A little cautious as well. Like she wanted to give him a chance but didn't really trust him yet.

But she wasn't scared of him either. That was good.

"All right. I'll do what I can."

"You're shtill shleeping in the cage," Bobby snarled, spittle flying from his mandibles. "Don't think you'll get the royal treatment."

He should've seen that coming he supposed. That was good, though. He could get his knife.

He knew they'd arrived at Bazyli's office when he saw Gerard waiting, leaning against the wall, as though waiting for them.

Acting as a backup in case John decided to do something.

Not a surprise. He was wearing a collar. He had no illusions he was being trusted here.

Time to go chat with his new boss.

The next evil scientist John would be a henchman for.

11

Matthew's dad was *pissed*.

"You went to the bar?" Bazyli's eyes flashed to a dangerous red. It wasn't as though Matthew had never seen that color on him before, but it never got easy.

Bazyli's anger was always intense.

"I wanted to get a feel for the people. It's been a while."

It didn't take long before he'd found out. Matthew had been stupid for thinking he could hide it from him.

Matthew had a great time at the Hub. He'd ended up sitting with TJ until closing. The man even talked him into playing that game of trivia. The guy had been curious when Matthew couldn't answer pretty much any of the questions. Even the ones he'd said were obvious.

How the hell was Matthew supposed to know who Michael Myers was and what that had to do with Halloween? There were apparently fictional characters out there who could shoot spider webs, fly, or turn into big green monsters.

And those were apparently not shifters.

TJ hadn't been a dick about it, though. He'd smiled and joked with Matthew, but it never seemed malicious.

"You don't watch a lot of movies, do you?"

Matthew had still felt embarrassed, trying to hide his face behind his drink. "No."

TJ had tilted his head just slightly, as though he didn't understand. But then looked as though he thought he did, clapping Matthew on the shoulder. "Don't worry. I got you. We'll win this."

First place got a meal for free. Second place, two free appetizers. Third place got two free drinks.

They got last place.

But it was fun. Matthew had learned so much.

Well, at least about trivia topics. He'd become so distracted that he'd forgotten his real reason for being there, and he hadn't gotten any relevant information from TJ about his procedures.

So now he was here, making up bullshit he was pretty sure his father could see right through.

"There are former patients of that *mother* woman who live in that town, and you need blood samples—"

"We have multiple of mother's experiments in our facility *right now,*" Bazyli snapped. "Bobby, Gerard, *and* John."

"But TJ was a failed experiment that FUC put to right," Matthew replied.

"I don't care!" Bazyli boomed. "You are *never* to be seen by the public. Not without *my* permission or protection."

"We're hiding down here like rats and getting almost nothing out of that snake you have in the basement," Matthew fought back. "And those flowers Rachel is growing aren't giving you any results."

That was apparently the wrong thing to say. Bazyli's eyes narrowed.

He was only a fox shifter, but there was a strength to him, a presence Matthew couldn't place. Like the man held Matthew's life in the palm of his hand and could squish it whenever he wanted.

Bazyli tapped his fingers on his worn desk before moving to the black cabinet next to it. He ran a finger carefully across the top.

"I've been given some information that indicates Bobby and Gerard can no longer be trusted."

Matthew wasn't entirely shocked. Bobby and Gerard were only here because they hoped Bazyli could fix them, and since he hadn't made any progress, it made sense their loyalty would wane.

He was only curious as to what they'd done that had finally caught Bazyli's attention, busy as he always seemed to be.

"What did they do?"

"Gerard has not been feeding the prisoner, and John has told me that Bobby has been making... some concerning observations about your sister."

Matthew didn't understand.

Then he thought he did. "Are you saying Rachel is in danger?"

Bazyli took a breath. He seemed deep in thought. Torn about something.

"It's a risk I am not comfortable taking. So I've decided to take a chance with John. He will work for me now."

"*What?*" Matthew couldn't believe it. "You're going to trust him to just... wander around? After everything?"

"He is to be monitored. I put a collar on him. Your sister

and Bobby are currently holding remotes for it. They will be here shortly."

"You won't trust me to go and get a drink at a bar, but you'll let that *snake* walk around?" Matthew couldn't hide his offense.

He didn't particularly hate John, but the man was dangerous. He'd grabbed and kissed Rachel in front of him, after all.

A fact that he should share with his father...

"That *snake* has more experience than the three of you combined," Bazyli continued. "He worked for that worthless *mother* woman in this area for quite a long time, proving himself loyal and useful. I could use someone like that."

Bazyli's sneer in Matthew's direction told him exactly what his father meant by that.

"Useful?" Matthew thought Bazyli was acting strange. This was... What would Rachel call it? Out of character.

Something else was happening. Something he wasn't mentioning to Matthew.

"Yes. Useful. He has no connections and nowhere to go. He's a fugitive in FUC's opinion. He'll find safety and protection here."

"Father, with all due respect, you don't know all the dangers he might pose here."

"Oh? Do you have something to tell me?"

Matthew opened his mouth to reveal that it might not be Bobby he should be worrying about when there was a knock on the door behind him.

"Enter," Bazyli called.

Rachel opened the door, peeking her head in, an easy smile pulling at her lips, which quickly vanished when she saw Matthew.

"Uh, Daddy, the boys are here."

Matthew rolled his eyes as Bobby and John walked in, Rachel tailing behind them.

John's face was almost entirely healed from the beating Matthew had given him. Now he had only minor bruising around his eyes and nose, along with the scars he'd arrived with.

But it was Bobby who interested him the most. He looked as though he'd been in a fistfight quit recently.

Matthew glanced back at Bazyli, noting the slight swell in his knuckles. He normally would have spotted that immediately, but he'd been distracted.

"Thank you for joining us, gentlemen," Bazyli said, looking at John. "My apologies for not being there when you woke up, but I had business to see to."

Matthew's face went hot when Bazyli glanced at him, but there was nothing he could do. Not now.

"No problem," John said, shooting a light glare at Matthew. "I guess you're hiring?"

"So to speak. My resources are... stretched thin, as you've seen. I need more hands, and it would simplify things if you would willingly give your blood. I don't enjoy putting you to sleep and on a table for my samples. It's much preferable to have an ally instead of an unwilling participant."

John's lips thinned. "Right. Makes sense."

Matthew did not like the way John glanced at Rachel. As if he'd already made up his mind and had his reasons why.

Matthew couldn't stand it. "Father, John is a threat. You cannot possibly trust him around Rachel." He looked at his sister. "Tell him!"

Rachel squared her shoulders. "I spoke to Daddy about that already."

What?

His shock must have shown on his face.

Even John no longer seemed as calm as he'd once been.

"I know John attempted to grab her in order to escape." Bazyli's eyes flashed red, glancing at John. "That's why she has a remote as well. I trust you will keep your hands to yourself now that you are no longer caged?"

"I wouldn't hurt her. Sir," John added, insisting with his full chest.

He sounded sincere, but Matthew was going to rip out his own hair. Father *knew*? And he was still signing off on this? When did Rachel tell him? *How* did she tell him?

"You can't be serious? You're going to take his word on this?"

"I need to have a word with my children." Bazyli pointed at the others and gestured toward the door. "You three. Get out. Bobby, wait."

Bobby stopped, glancing back at Bazyli, who held out his hand. "Give me the remote. You were only meant to hold it temporarily."

Bobby's spine stiffened, outrage playing out across his eyes. He grumbled under his breath, reaching into his pocket and producing the remove. A small thing that could fit on a keychain or lanyard. Grey in color with a single button.

He slammed it onto the desk.

John hissed suddenly.

The button must have been pushed slightly when he did that.

No matter. The shock seemed to be over quickly, and the three men walked out.

John hesitated at the door, glancing back at them. No doubt wondering what was going to be said about him when he was gone. That was too damn bad.

When the door shut, Matthew pointed at it, unable to stop himself. "You can't be serious about this."

"I am perfectly serious in my duties," Bazyli hissed, rising to his feet, his hands pressing down on the old wood. "Unlike you, who went out in the night, drinking and wasting time like a common fool."

Matthew's face burned. He thought of TJ as they drank. Matthew had a soda, because he had no ID, and TJ had a beer. Both laughed as though Matthew was just as inebriated as TJ over some joke he couldn't remember.

"You told me there is nothing wasted when information is gathered."

"And what information have you gathered while you leave your sister here, unattended? I found her on the surface while you were gone. I trusted you both more than that."

Matthew snapped his attention to Rachel, who had the good grace to look ashamed.

She'd gone to the surface?

"What were you doing?"

"Letting my panda out." She glared down at her feet. "You all get to do it. I needed to exercise. "

"You can exercise down here. If you need sunlight, then tend to the flowers. That is your job."

Rachel looked about ready to cry, so Matthew turned the heat back on himself. "If you're letting John into our ranks because I haven't been here, then I swear to you, Father, I will not go to the bar anymore."

"You could have been recognized."

"How? I've never been in any FUC database. I'm not one of *Mother's* prisoners. Who would recognize me?"

Bazyli slammed a fist on his desk. Everything on it jumped.

Rachel jumped a little, too. Matthew didn't move, feeling oddly detached from his Father's wrath.

"Do not argue with me," Bazyli said. "Do not go back there. You are never to be seen by those people. Ever."

Matthew got that feeling again. That Bazyli was hiding something.

Matthew didn't like that feeling. He trusted his father, and Matthew wasn't smart enough to understand much of what he did.

Wrong. That uncomfortable twisting in his gut was misplaced, that was all. Had to be. And yet, he couldn't bring himself to ask Bazyli point-blank if he knew that John had kissed Rachel, either.

Maybe his father really did know. Maybe the old fox was using his own daughter to keep the snake around and cooperating.

"I won't go anymore," Matthew said, the words tasting like a lie in his mouth.

Bazyli nodded then looked at Rachel. "And you? Now that you have some assistance and protection, you will not be on the surface any longer?"

Rachel nodded. "Yes, sir."

Bazyli picked up the remote on his desk, handing it to Matthew.

"Take this. I don't trust either of those other two idiots with it."

He shouldn't trust Matthew with it either, but Matthew pocketed the thing.

Suddenly, Bazyli just looked tired. Worn out. Matthew wished he understood why.

"Daddy?" Rachel asked.

He waved her off. "Just... tend to those flowers for me,

will you, sweet? We're close. So close to duplicating what FUC has done."

"What if we asked FUC for help?" Matthew asked, knowing his mistake a second later when Bazyli sneered at him.

"How many times have I told you?" Bazyli asked, his shoulder sagging. "They would shut down my research. Destroy everything. Even your sister. Do you want them to hurt your sister?"

Matthew couldn't imagine someone like TJ wanting to lay a finger on Rachel.

But what did he really know about TJ? They'd shared some drinks and played a few games. That was it.

Matthew was being stupid. Bazyli was right.

He squared his shoulders. "Sorry, sir."

Bazyli huffed an impatient noise. He looked at Rachel, his gaze sad.

Rachel's shoulders sagged. She played with a loose string on her dress. "I'm sorry, Daddy."

Bazyli nodded. He walked around to the other side of his desk, in front of Rachel. She flinched a little when he touched her face.

"I'm sorry, sweetheart," he said.

Rachel's lower lip trembled. She threw herself into his chest, hugging him tightly.

Bazyli seemed thrown off by this, but he held her.

It was almost warm to watch. Matthew, though he was their family, felt like an intruder for seeing it.

Bazyli looking so vulnerable. It was strange.

Until Bazyli stroked Rachel's red hair, his lips twisting, expression turning sour. Disgust, so brief Matthew would have missed it if he'd blinked, there and gone in an instant.

Was there something in her hair? Matthew couldn't see anything that would have made Bazyli react that way.

"That's enough of that." The warmth of the moment vanished. Bazyli took Rachel's shoulders and gently, but firmly, pushed her back, clearing his throat. "Go and tend to our lilies. I need to proceed with my next experiment. Don't fail me again, either of you."

"A-all right, Daddy," Rachel said.

Matthew nodded, his brain turning over everything he'd just seen as he and Rachel took their leave from Bazyli's office.

Gerard, Bobby, and John were all outside, as though waiting for them.

Rachel smiled a little too warmly at John for Matthew's liking.

"Did *Daddy* give you both a spanking?" Bobby mocked.

"No, he had his fill with you," Rachel shot back, shocking Matthew. Rachel didn't normally speak like that.

His father was acting strange. Rachel was acting strange. And John...

Matthew would have to keep an eye on him. He didn't like the way the man smiled at his sister, as if he was equally impressed by her words.

Thankfully, that smile vanished when John realized Matthew was looking at him.

Matthew was tempted to pull out the little remote and give it a test right then and there, but he refrained. He didn't need to be smart, or a mind reader, to know John was remembering what it felt like when Matthew held him down and beat him for daring to put his hands on Rachel.

He'd get more of the same if he tried that again.

12

Rachel loved her brother dearly, but after several days of his hovering, she had to admit, she was getting sick of it.

"You don't have to babysit me," she said. It was time for some of the lilies to be cut. Their red and white petals would be dried in a machine then ground into a fine powder for lab use. "I *am* older than you, you know. I might have even babysat you a time or two when we were smaller."

"I doubt that," Matthew said. "You look barely a year older than me."

Rachel had to give him that. The truth was, neither of them quite knew how old they were. And sometimes, Matthew even looked older than her.

She pushed passed her brother, her tray of petals in her hand as she put them into the dehydrator. A machine with several shelves inside. It would take a few hours, but the petals would be what was needed for the next experiment.

Whatever that was.

She felt bad for cutting them, however. They were pretty. She'd watered them, cared for them, and they'd kept her company when she was lonely.

"I'm just curious about what this is all about."

"You're bored," she said. "And you're watching me."

Something that annoyed Rachel greatly. John stood off in the corner, a pair of clippers in his hand as he gently snipped off some leaves.

And flower heads.

Rachel hadn't had a moment alone with John since this new arrangement had started.

Though the good news was that she'd also barely seen Bobby or Gerard.

Bazyli had been determined to put them to work, and while it meant she was still trapped down here, watching the flowers, doing her job, there was a significant weight lifted from her shoulders.

"I have reason to be concerned." Matthew glanced toward John. "You know why."

"I'm not going to grab her again, if that's what you're worried about," John said, sounding as tired of this whole thing as Rachel felt.

His choice of words was interesting, considering Rachel had been thinking of that kiss non-stop since it happened.

She maybe, sort of, kind of, wouldn't mind it if he did kiss her again.

"You couldn't put your hands on her if you tried," Matthew said. "I'd stop you, and if I wasn't around, she'd give you a shock herself."

Rachel grabbed the little remote hanging around her neck. Matthew had tied it with an old shoelace he'd found, as though making sure for himself that she would always have it on her.

It was sweet, but the more time that passed, the more Rachel was convinced John was not a threat.

"Yeah, yeah," John said.

The first two days with his new collar on him he'd seemed to take Matthew's threats more seriously.

Now, he shrugged them off, barely giving them any sort of attention.

"Matthew, go to the surface. Father's been in his lab for two days. He won't notice if you're gone for a few hours."

And it would give her more time to be alone with John.

Matthew looked outraged. "I do not need to go to the surface and leave you alone here with him!"

"He's not going to hurt me. You said so yourself."

"Not because I trust him," Matthew said. "His skin isn't poison, fine, we were wrong, but he still bites."

John chose that moment to jump in, holding a tray of leaves, flower heads, petals, and pollen that needed to be dried. "You still believe that bullshit lie that my skin was ever poison? That's cute."

Matthew's neck went tight. He shook his head, his hands clenching into fists.

Rachel's face became unbearably hot.

She hadn't been poisoned when John kissed her. She was embarrassed to think of the way she'd panicked, but there was... something.

His mouth on hers had pushed something into her mind and body she could not shake even to this day.

Even now, seeing him holding the tray of flowers, his sleeves rolled up to his elbows, which showed off the muscle of his tanned forearms...

She'd *never* had thoughts like these before.

Not that she could remember, anyway.

If they'd been wrong about John, or if Bobby and the others had lied, then it gave her a few other things to think about as well.

Things she couldn't get into with Matthew insisting on standing right there, constantly hovering.

"Go outside. I know you want to."

"Dad's not letting us," Matthew said. "You know that."

This was a risk, but she'd had to take it. "TJ might want to have another game tonight."

Matthew's whole body seemed to straighten up. "What? What are you—"

"I checked your burner phone. I'm sorry!" she added quickly, genuinely feeling bad, but she had been curious at the sight of him constantly pulling it out, sending those messages. "I knew you were texting too much for it to be with Bobby or Gerard."

The person he was texting had to be a good friend. Matthew's reading was improving as well since this TJ person insisted on texting with proper spelling.

Matthew seemed to like it whenever he got texts from TJ.

Matthew glared at her. The genuine betrayal she saw on his face was... to be expected.

"You went through my things?"

"You should maybe be more careful about it," she said, taking a step back when his anger didn't simmer down. "I won't do it again, but if you've made a friend, you should go and see him."

"He's not a friend. I'm watching him. He's a cadet."

"A cadet?" John asked. "Named TJ?"

Rachel had almost forgotten about him. He was still holding his tray with the flower petals, but his gaze seemed far away.

"Yeah," Matthew said. "Did you know him?"

John shook his head. "Not really. I left before... everything. He was one of the guys Mother messed up. I'd heard he got treated. Fixed. Is he really walking around now? Looking... normal?"

"I guess." Matthew shrugged.

Rachel hadn't thought about how the mention of Matthew's friend would impact John. Despite everything, it was easy to forget his connection to the people of FUCN'A.

"Leave the guy alone." John suddenly sent a cool, steely stare at Matthew. "He's been through enough."

"I'm not doing anything," Matthew objected.

"You're trying to either dig information out of him or put him in a cage like your Daddy did to me. To get his blood for tests."

"Not like FUC has been quick to share their information with us," Matthew snapped back. "They'd sooner kill us than help us."

"What?" John fell back a step, his eyes wide. "*That's* what you think?"

"What else should we think? Look at Bobby," Matthew demanded. "They'd let Bobby rot because he's not nice enough or whatever. I *know* there were others."

"People who kidnapped and tortured other people so they could have people to experiment on," John replied. "Bobby volunteered because... I actually don't know why, but he willingly got himself into this with a crazy person, and look where that got him!"

"So he should be made to suffer for the rest of his life?" Matthew spat back.

Rachel was shocked. She'd never heard her brother defend Bobby like this.

Then she was proud.

Matthew was right. Bobby wasn't always nice, and, well, neither was Gerard, but they had their reasons. They didn't deserve to suffer.

"Do you think Matthew and I chose this?" she asked.

"I don't know what's going on with the two of you. Honestly? Matthew, you look familiar. I can't place it, but it's like we've met before. Or maybe I know someone who looks like you."

"What?" Matthew blinked as if he hadn't seen that coming.

Rachel sure hadn't.

John shrugged. "Maybe you've just got one of those faces, but I've seen a lot of other people being worked on. I've been wondering, how do you really know if that man is your father? Do either of you remember anything about your lives?"

"He's my dad," Rachel said, feeling a terrible heat rising inside herself. "He's my dad. I know it."

She wanted to put an end to this line of thinking. She no longer wanted to ask John any questions. She suddenly didn't want to know what he would say if this was the sort of thing that would come out of his stupid mouth.

"But *how* do you know?" John pressed.

"That's a stupid question to ask!"

"No, it's not!" John shot back. "Do you have any idea how many people got taken for a ride by guys like him? By shifters who're trying to experiment on people?"

Rachel was furious. This wasn't what she wanted. She didn't want him to talk about her father.

Her dad loved her. He loved Matthew. She *knew* he did.

"You don't know what you're talking about," she said.

Matthew's burner phone, the one Rachel had admitted to snooping through just a moment ago, suddenly vibrated in the pocket of Matthew's old jacket.

He yanked it out with a growl and looked at the message, the color vanishing from his face. "I... I gotta go."

He took one step toward the door and stopped, looking at Rachel and John like he was having some sort of crisis.

Rachel didn't understand. "What's the matter?"

"Nothing. Dad's calling me. I have to... Will you be...?"

Rachel understood. She pulled the remote she wore from under her shirt, showing him she still had it. "I'll be fine. Go. I'm sure it's important."

Just as she was also sure it wasn't their father who was summoning him.

She hoped TJ was all right. Matthew seemed to get along with him well, but something was wrong if the way Matthew flew out of here was anything to go by.

Matthew shot John one last, desperate stare.

"I won't touch her," John promised.

That seemed to be enough. Whatever it was, Matthew ran out of there like there was a fire licking at his feet.

Leaving her alone with John.

It was strange, for the first few seconds, being just the two of them together and no one else.

She looked at John.

He stared back at her. "Are you scared of me?"

She didn't have to think too deeply about it. "No."

He nodded. "That's good to know, but can I ask why? You barely know me. I have done some bad things."

Rachel nodded. "Yes, well, no one's perfect. Matthew and I are thieves. We steal things. I suppose... I don't know. You don't scare me." She made sure he could see that she had the remote as well. "Especially not when I'm holding this."

He grinned. "Fair enough." His eyes flashed. "I won't talk about your dad if you don't want me to."

"I don't."

He nodded. "So, what did you want to talk about?" His voice was soft. He stood close while keeping out of grabbing distance. She knew he could move quickly, but despite it, she trusted him.

And there was the fact that something in the way he spoke did something to her. As though his voice caressed her skin, putting her at ease and wrapping her up in its sound and warmth.

Rachel's heart slammed. She was about to ask so many questions. About the outside world. About other shifters.

A lot of which might fly in the face of the things her father had told her.

Was she ready? Could she do it?

She took a deep breath.

13

Matthew considered taking the truck. The one that was only permitted to be used for certain tasks. Usually involving a pickup or a supply run. Otherwise, they didn't want it on the road very often.

Bazyli was always good about keeping the things they did secret. He'd made it clear, again and again, that he had no intentions of drawing attention to himself the same way other scientists had.

The truck was not in the garage, but luckily, Matthew didn't need one when he could fly. He packed in his clothes and phone in the bag that he could easily clutch in his owl talons.

He didn't have to go far, and it seemed, the call was only a short flight down the road.

What the hell those two idiots thought they were doing messing around in the middle of the day was something Matthew had to deal with later. They weren't supposed to be out here. He had to get them back before someone saw them.

The fact that TJ was sitting in the back of the truck,

hands tied behind his back, while Bobby and Gerard yelled at each other, trying desperately to change a flat tire, was the thing he was most focused on.

What the hell was *he* doing here?

TJ looked up and watched as Matthew flew toward him, and the cadet's eyes bulged damn near out of his sockets at the bear-sized owl that swooped in for a landing.

Matthew stared back at him, his heart sinking.

"What took you sho long?" Bobby slurred, his face and mandibles red. A couple of veins popped out at the side of his head. "Come help ush with thish!"

He was not in a good mood. Not that Matthew could blame him.

Matthew could not help them. He could grab TJ right now and fly away with him, drop him off somewhere safe.

But that would risk Matthew being seen and followed back to their underground lab. They would ruin what Bazyli was trying to do. They would destroy the medicine he was making for Bobby and Gerard. They'd take Matthew's and Rachel's shifting abilities away and lock Bazyli up.

"What are you waiting for!" Gerard snapped. "Get over here!"

Decision made, Matthew shifted, letting himself become human again. Letting TJ see him.

If TJ looked shocked at the sight of an over-sized saber-toothed owl, it was nothing compared to when he saw Matthew himself.

Matthew couldn't look back at him.

Shame washed through him as he yanked his pants out of his bag, getting them on. "It's a flat tire. What's the problem?"

Bobby, who managed to calm down slightly, explained the issue. He could work well enough with computers, but it seemed he and Gerard were helpless when it came to switching out a tire.

Matthew could do it. Easily. It was one of the skills he'd learned after walking, talking, feeding and dressing himself, after Bazyli cured him of that sickness he'd had.

The one that robbed him of his memories.

He'd been able to read a motor and change tires before he could read words.

"Found this one snooping around," Bobby said. He looked at the back of the cab, almost seeming... regretful. "Never thought I'd see him again."

"You're bringing him back to the compound?" Matthew asked as he began changing the tire.

"Have to. Can't let him go. He shaw me." Bobby's mandibles twitched.

Matthew glanced at the truck bed.

TJ seemed to be staring at nothing in particular, his eyes in a wide panic, mouth gagged.

Matthew didn't want to do this. He didn't know the guy that well, but he was nice. He didn't deserve this.

"You should have blindfolded him," Matthew said, grunting as he dealt with the lug nuts "Even if he saw you, that doesn't mean anything."

"It means lots when he's working for FUC now!" Bobby yanked something out of his pocket, throwing it at Matthew.

It hit his arm. He barely managed to catch it before it could fall to the ground.

He looked at the image of TJ on the badge. "So? He's a cadet. He's in training, not on a mission."

"Shame difference!" Bobby snarled, getting worked up again and slurring his words. "He'll turn ush in! He got to be fixshed because he wash their favorite!"

"Okay, okay." Matthew shoved the badge in his pocket and went back to changing the tire.

"He'sh no better than ush! He did shit before too!"

"I believe you. Fine," Matthew said, irritated and getting sucked into Bobby's tantrum. "Let's just get him back. Maybe Bazyli will see if he can be useful to us."

"On a table. Fuck him," Bobby said.

"Seriously?" Gerard asked. "What did he do to you?"

"Fuck you!" Bobby snapped. "You done with that tire yet or what?"

Matthew took a breath, tightening the last lug nut. "Yeah. I'm done. I'll ride in the back with him.

He tossed the popped tire and tools into the back of the truck before climbing into the bed. He barely sat his ass down next to TJ before the man shocked him by punching him in the face.

He must have somehow gotten his hands untied.

Gerard cursed, he and Bobby scrambling out of the cab, but they shouldn't have bothered.

Matthew had TJ by the wrists and pinned in a second. He was much bigger than the guy was.

"Stop fighting. You're just going to make it worse."

TJ shook his head, glaring at him. "Fuck you," he said, his words muffled heavily through the gag.

For some reason, that got Matthew right in the damn heart.

"Give me another zip tie," he shouted to the others.

Gerard scrambled to the back, returning with another one.

"Put your hands in front of you," Matthew said.

TJ shook his head.

Matthew had to force himself to be calm. If he flew off

the handle, TJ could panic and keep fighting, and someone would get hurt.

"Do as I say, or I'll break your wrists." He squeezed just enough to make it painful, to prove that he meant it.

TJ's golden amber eyes widened. Matthew noticed that he had long eyelashes for a guy.

Thankfully, he let his hands be put in front of him, allowed himself to be tied again.

Matthew knew that if someone could break a zip tie with their hands behind them, then they could certainly do it with their hands in front of them, too.

At least this way he could keep an eye on things.

"Get us out of here," he said to Bobby, feeling tired.

He couldn't look at TJ.

The guy who'd laughed with him, but not at him, for not knowing all those pop culture facts.

The guy who texted him back and forth, asking when he would be back and if they could hang out again.

He didn't want to see any of the betrayal on his face.

And he didn't want to feel like a bigger piece of shit than he already felt.

The truck moved.

Matthew could only hope that this wasn't going to turn into some horrible disaster for them all.

It took everything he had not to stick his face in his hands on the ride back home.

14

John had to be careful with his words when he spoke to Rachel. He didn't trust her father, that fox, as far as he could throw the man, but Rachel loved him.

He was, until proven otherwise, her father, after all.

So John had to change his tactics. He had to get her to see that, despite the faults that FUC had, they at least weren't the ones experimenting on people against their will.

Nor were they an organization that *exterminated* those who'd been illegally experimented on.

"Okay, but they put you in a cage," Rachel reasoned.

"Because I was helping an evil scientist," he said. "And I kidnapped a kid at her behest."

He glanced at Rachel. She flinched at the mention of child abduction, as though the very thought of something so awful put a sour taste in her mouth.

She already knew this, but he needed her to understand that it wasn't FUC she needed to be worried about.

Rachel glanced at him with something uncomfortable in her eyes. That warmth she sometimes looked at him with was nowhere to be found as he reminded her of what a piece of shit he was.

He didn't blame her in the slightest.

He was never going to think back on that time in his life without a massive cringe.

"Is the child okay?"

John nodded. "Yeah, the baby was fine. The woman I was working for... Well, she had problems. I think she lost her own children, so whenever she brought anyone in, she called us her children. She wanted us all to be a big family."

"So she took someone's baby?"

"Albert and Beverly's baby." John winced, knowing the whole thing was morbid as fuck. "I try to say their names, so they're real people to me. So I remember what I did to real people. The woman bossing me around, though... I never even knew her name. Anyway, she wanted an actual child, I think. A baby she could raise." He shook his head. "I couldn't do it. Volunteering to get experimented on, or even talking other people into it, was one thing. Taking someone's kid..."

He shook his head, the shame washing through the underside of his skin like acid, eating away at him. Forever and ever.

"You gave the baby back, though, right?"

"Yes." He looked at her sharply.

Rachel stared back at him as the flower petals continued to dry in the machine. She'd pulled herself up to sit on one of the metal tables, her legs dangling off the floor.

She looked at him like there was no doubt in her mind that he'd done it, that he'd at least given that boy back to his mother and father.

She smiled. "Good."

He took a breath.

This was more than he'd ever hoped for. This accep-tance, the immediate belief that he wasn't some fucking monster.

Though it felt wonderful to have it, an instant later, it rotted inside him. He didn't fucking deserve it.

"Yeah, I gave the kid back," he said then pointed at all the scars on his face. "The father did this to me when he got his hands on me, though."

Her smile faltered. She shuddered.

"Do you blame him?" He had to know. He *had* to know.

She seemed to think about that then shook her head. "I suppose not, but... you're still a good person."

What the fuck? Why was she doing this to him? Why did she insist on filling him up with this *forgiveness*?

He almost laughed. He had to turn away, looking down at the variety of leaves, vines, petals, and pollen that were being turned into powders and potions for Rachel's father to use.

"What's the matter?"

"I'm starting to understand why your brother worries about you." He looked at her. The little remote dangled around her neck when she should be keeping that thing firmly in her hands at all times.

She frowned. "Why?"

"Because you trust too much." He thought about that quickly. "Actually, the both of you do. Even the way you defend Bobby is going to get you in trouble."

"Bobby's been through a lot."

"Yes, at the hands of people who don't mind getting dirty." He looked at her pointedly. "Your father works with the same type. They're all sharing information *and* manpower."

Rachel's lovely pink lips thinned. He hated to see her look so upset.

She didn't defend her father this time, however. She took a breath. "So, are you saying my dad also experimented on you?"

"Not personally," John said, shrugging. "But if the woman I was working for was associated with your father. Then he had a hand in what happened to Bobby." He pushed around a few of the crushed petals on his tray, wondering what exactly these were going to be used for.

"Do you think Bobby knows?"

John snapped his attention over to her.

Rachel seemed lost in thought.

"Do *you* think he knows?" John had to ask.

Rachel's red hair was wild around her shoulders. She seemed a little embarrassed, pushing some of it behind her ear.

She shook her head.

Grief filled him. For her. For the questions she was asking and the fact that he was, little by little, ripping away the few layers of innocence a person like her could have in the situation she was in.

"I don't think he knows either," John said.

Rachel tapped her fingers on the metal table. She seemed to be thinking about so many different things at the same time.

He didn't want her to spiral. He knew what that felt like, getting sucked into a such a tsunami of emotions and revelations that hours could go by before he surfaced.

He needed to keep her here, with him.

"You said your dad loves you and Matthew though, right?"

Rachel jumped a little, blinking, as though she'd been

falling right into that pit of endless information and terror, just to be yanked back at the last second.

"He does." She swallowed and straightened her back a little. "I know he does."

He nodded. "Okay, I believe you."

The guy was rough when he was angry, but sometimes parents were. It wasn't good, but it didn't mean he didn't care.

In his own way.

"So there's got to be something good in this. You said he was doing all this because you and Matthew were sick?"

Rachel nodded, that light coming back into her eyes, hope returning for her father's soul.

"Yeah. We were dying. Shifters have the ability to heal, and they don't suffer the same illnesses that humans do. So he needed to turn us."

"What were you sick with?"

He didn't mean to dig, didn't want to lead her down another rabbit hole, but his question seemed to do just that, as Rachel's smile slowly melted away.

"I... I don't know. We were sick. We had the same disease."

"Right," he said gently. "But do you know what that was? Did he ever tell you?"

Rachel shook her head. "Matthew and I can't remember our lives. I woke up first. Matthew had it the worst. He had to learn how to walk and talk and just do everything all over again. It was like he was a toddler."

"Huh." John rubbed his hand over the back of his neck, all the bad vibes flaring up in the back of his head.

Of course something felt off about this. This whole situation was a shitshow.

"Have you heard of that before?"

He shook his head. "I've heard of people who were taken, experimented on when they were just little kids. People who practically grew up in the labs, but they were treated like lab rats. Not like the main bad guy's children."

"My father's not a bad guy," Rachel said immediately.

"Right, sorry, sorry." He had to give it to her. She was loyal. She definitely loved that damn fox.

It was a shame the bastard didn't deserve it.

John needed to get off this topic. He didn't want to get on her nerves or raise her defenses. That wouldn't work if he needed her to think about the situation she was in.

"Can I ask you something?"

The dehydrating machine next to her dinged. Rachel hopped neatly off the table and opened it, grabbing some oven mitts before taking the tray out.

Turning her back to him. Totally trusting.

"Sure," she said.

"You have no idea who I am. You only have my word on a lot of this, and you thought I was poisonous to touch not too long ago. Why do you trust me enough to let me work with you?"

Rachel set the tray aside, removed her mitts, and closed the machine.

She took a breath, holding the mitts in both hands, looking at him.

"You have that collar on you, but I know my father wouldn't take a risk with me. He thinks I'm fragile." She seemed to think about that. "I guess I am. I'm not like Matthew, Bobby, or Gerard. I'm not very strong, and my animal form is nice. I love being a red panda. I think they're cute."

John thought they were cute, too.

"But the others can do more than I can. They're faster, and Matthew can fly."

He waited for her to finish. If he was honest, he felt a little of the same. Envy toward the larger, more capable shifters.

And also protective toward Rachel. He didn't want her going out in the world and putting herself at risk when she didn't need to either. He wanted to keep her safe. He wanted to protect her from the hurt in the world.

Which was a strange thing to feel, considering how much the truth he wanted her to know and believe so badly would crush her.

"If my father can feel like that and still be all right with you around me, then it means he doesn't think you're a threat."

John blinked. "Seriously?" He almost laughed. It was kind of embarrassing. "You're fine with being near me because your dad *approves* of me?"

She grinned, shrugging one shoulder. "Maybe. I keep telling you he's not a bad man." Then her smile faltered. "You did some bad things, so... if he did, too, will you forgive him?"

Fuck him sideways. How was he supposed to get defensive when she asked him something like that? "Maybe. I guess it depends on whether or not he's sorry."

Did that even matter? And what right did John have to judge someone when he'd been just as bad? This was all so fucked.

"What about the poison thing? You were lied to about that."

"I'm not so sure that you aren't poisonous."

He didn't understand. Then he thought he did. John grinned. "I made your knees go weak when I kissed you."

She didn't look back at him.

Holy shit.

Holy. Shit.

He was fucking right. The knowledge excited him. He laughed. "I thought you were being dramatic. When I kissed you—"

"Which was a rude thing to do, by the way."

"Yes, it was," he said right away. "And your big bro got me back for that in spades, but when you went down, I kind of thought you were being a little dramatic."

She whirled on him. "*Dramatic?*"

He grinned. Nodding. "That wasn't it, though. Your knees went weak. I made you *swoon*!"

The word felt foreign coming out of his mouth, and it tasted fucking sweet on his tongue, too. He'd made a woman do an honest-to-God swoon.

With all the shitty things that had been happening to him over the last several months, this had to be the highlight.

Rachel's face turned a bright shade of red. She had that pursed-lip look that made her look... adorable.

He wanted to kiss her again.

He took a step closer.

She frowned, casting her eyes up and down, sizing him up. "What are you doing?"

"Put the remote in your hand."

"Why?"

"Just do it."

She was clearly confused, but interested. She fumbled for the little remote hanging around her neck. She gripped it tightly in her left hand, staring at him, waiting. His heart thudded heavily. He wasn't sure whether he was worried she would shock him...

Or reject him.

"Just do me a favor. Don't click the button unless you absolutely want to."

"O-okay," she said.

He took another step forward. Rachel's shoulders bunched up, but she quickly relaxed.

Then he took another step, and another, until he stood toe to toe with her, looking down at her.

It honestly wouldn't take much for him to grab her hand and take the remote from her. Even as she held it in a tight fist.

He didn't want to do that, however.

He wanted to see if she would choose this.

He could hear the sound of her heart hammering, a heavy pulse in her throat and chest, and wrists as he reached for her.

His fingers slid to the back of her hair. His other hand held her shoulder. He kept his hold light. He didn't grip her at all.

John glanced down and to the side, at the remote she held. Her finger was right over the button.

He grinned at her. "You sure I'm not made of poison?"

She blinked several times, as though coming out of a dream. "You... you're touching me right now."

He supposed he was. "Not skin to skin. My hand's on your shoulder, and the other is in your hair."

Would touching her hair count? The air in here suddenly felt warm between them again.

He could tell she felt it too. Her chest rose and fell with each quick breath.

He couldn't stop looking at her lips. She licked them, leaving behind a soft, wet sheen.

He groaned, his breath catching. "Why'd you have to go and do that?"

He kissed her quick. He couldn't stop himself, but then, the threat of that damn remote, and the shock he'd get if he startled her, caused him to pull away.

He looked into her eyes. Their faces were close enough that their noses almost touched.

"That feel like poison to you?"

Rachel swallowed. Her body trembled.

"No," she said. "But it felt good."

The remote dropped from her hand. It would have clattered to the floor had she not been wearing it around her neck.

Not that he noticed or cared when she threw her arms around his shoulders and kissed him full on the mouth.

15

That burning, tingling feeling came back. It consumed her like the water that went above her head. Like a fire that whooshed and breathed and swirled around her.

Crazy that she could want more of that, but she did.

And since Matthew was finally gone, it was so, so easy to let her body take over, giving in to what her body ached for.

John's lips against hers felt like nothing she'd ever experienced before. Then the touch of his tongue sent such a shock through her body that she groaned.

Rachel had to pull back. She had to take a breath.

"All good?" John asked, his forehead pressed against hers.

Rachel nodded. "Yeah. Yeah, that's...perfect."

She kissed him again. This feeling was addictive. She couldn't get enough of it. Like some instinct was taking over.

Had she done this before? With someone else? Before her memories had been lost?

Maybe, but Rachel couldn't imagine whatever she'd done in the past could have felt half as good as what she was doing now.

More. More. More.

John slid a hand down her flank to her waist and then the underside of her ass and thigh.

Somehow, she knew what he wanted her to do, and it only made sense as she groaned and lifted her leg, curling it around his lower back.

Then, to her immense shock, and pleasure, John's other hand slid down to her other leg.

He pulled her up and into his arms as if she weighed nothing at all, holding her tight, her thighs squeezing around his waist. He set her back on the metal table she'd been sitting on two seconds ago.

Distantly, Rachel heard something metal clatter to the floor.

That didn't matter.

She wanted to touch his skin. She *needed* it. It was the most important thing in the world to get her hands under his clothes.

Like an addiction.

He *was* poison. His touch might not kill her, but it ensnared her and corrupted her for anyone else.

She was completely hypnotized and taken by him.

She also felt the stiffness between her legs. It didn't startle her, which convinced her further that this wasn't a situation she was new to.

Which meant he really wasn't her first kiss. Just the first man she could remember kissing.

Matthew and Bazyli might think she was a precious little princess, but she had experienced this. Even if she couldn't remember her life before her sickness and the shifting, in this, she could be a little confidant.

A little naughty.

She might have thought twice about the whole thing

had she not been enjoying herself so thoroughly, had it not felt so amazing to grab a fistful of his hair and grip tight.

He groaned against her mouth, the warmth of his breath floating across her skin.

As hot and heavy as the kissing had started, it slowed down softly, as though someone had taken their foot off the gas pedal and just let the car they were driving roll to a stop.

Rachel still had to catch her breath. She was a little embarrassed, her forehead pressed against his, his hand pushed into her hair, fingers gentle on her scalp.

She could see the collar he wore clearly.

The fact that he was still a prisoner, kind of, suddenly bothered her. "Do you want me to take it off?"

His shoulders tensed. John's face turned bright red. "What? Really?"

She immediately understood, feeling her sudden embarrassment mirroring his own. "Your collar! I meant... your collar."

But the idea of what he was thinking about didn't seem bad. She wouldn't mind.

A quick glance down and she could see he was hard. That made her shockingly pleased. He was like *that*... for *her*.

"Oh!" John laughed, something both embarrassed, and disappointed, radiating from him. "I don't think I could get away with taking it off. Someone would notice."

"Right." Rachel couldn't stand the sight of it anymore though, especially not with John standing between her legs, her body wrapped around his.

It didn't feel right. It seemed... wrong.

"Don't feel bad," John said as if he was reading her mind. Then he gave her butt a playful squeeze. "You planning on shocking me?"

She couldn't help but return his smile. "Not so long as you're this nice to me."

"I'll always be nice to you."

There was something in the way he said it that gave her pause. She couldn't entirely figure it out, but they just looked at each other for a few, long seconds.

Rachel wasn't sure what she could say to that. John looked embarrassed for having said it.

As if he'd revealed a secret truth he wasn't prepared to make known.

She opened her mouth, but whatever she was going to say was immediately cut off by the banging sounds deeper in the compound.

The old, garage door on the level above them screeched open and then shut. The engine of the truck was killed.

And the distinct sound of shouting. From her brother, Gerard, and Bobby.

She and John looked at the ceiling then at each other.

"That what it normally sounds like when they come back?"

"No." She shook her head.

The mood was officially killed, and considering how high he'd pushed up the hem of her dress, Rachel figured that might be for the best as she pushed him away and jumped off the table, smoothing her clothes.

"We need to go see what's happening." She gestured for him to follow her, stopping for a moment on their way out. "Don't tell my brother what we just did."

He grinned, looking a little dashing and even mischievous with that naughty expression, his hair in disarray from Rachel gripping it.

"When I want your brother to smash my face in again, I'll tell him. Until then, it's our secret."

Rachel had to cover her mouth to hold in a laugh.

Then it was down to business. Finding out what had her brother, along with Gerard and Bobby, so upset.

———

HONESTLY, if Matthew were to find out what John had been doing with his sister, the beating would be worth it.

John's whole body felt warm, for one of the first times since he'd been in this damp little dungeon. Even the heat from the UV lamps in Rachel's garden didn't compare.

He wasn't even worried about what he would find when Rachel brought him upstairs to the garage.

Which was the closest he'd gotten to the outside world since he was dragged down here.

It was practically on the surface. A wide, open space that smelled of oil, the floor angled, upward slightly, the garage door shut, and no doubt hidden from sight on the outside.

He thought he would feel a need to run to it. To see if there was a way to open it, to get away.

Not without Rachel. His mind and body were completely settled on the idea that he couldn't leave without her.

Even with the collar around his neck, it felt easy, knowing he was choosing to stay.

In the garage, John spotted a dark blue van with all its tires missing and the truck, which Matthew, Gerard, and Bobby surrounded.

All three of them shouted at each other and looked to be at the razor's edge of a fistfight.

Matthew held on to the collar of Bobby's shirt. Gerard, who John had learned liked to pretend to be tougher than he was, stood off to the side. His already bulging eyes were wider than ever before.

"What are you doing?" Rachel rushed forward, grabbing Matthew's shoulder.

John didn't understand what everyone's problem was until he looked in the behind the cab and saw...

No way.

No. Fucking. Way.

"Hey, *hey!*" John surged forward running toward the man he recognized who was tied up in the bed of the truck.

The shouting stopped. John didn't expect his voice to carry the way it did in the garage. Or for everyone to suddenly look at him.

"What's going on here? How the hell did... Where did he come from?"

"Was shnooping around. Looking for shomething." Bobby glared at Matthew. "I had to."

This wasn't supposed to happen. It wasn't as though John knew TJ that well, but he had been part of the same group of people experimented on by John's previous boss.

John had seen him plenty of times, had seen the way his long, needle-pointed teeth had stretched and stabbed his gums. His eyes had been almost as buggy and big as Gerard's...

But the rumors were true. TJ looked normal now. He looked fine. He looked like a guy who had no business being here and getting involved in anything after what had happened to him.

TJ's eyes landed on John, and he did a double take. Then he glared something fierce at John.

Fuck. Goddamnit. Fuck!

"Why wasn't he blindfolded?" John sure as hell was when he'd been brought in. He could almost still feel that black bag that had been thrown over his head, the darkness and suffocation of it. It had barely been a few weeks ago.

"That's what I said!" Matthew snapped, his eyes a bright shade of red. John looked closer. Bobby had the collar of Matthew's shirt in his fists, but where Matthew gripped him back on his biceps, the hooked talons of his inner owl had emerged.

This was going to be a disaster.

"Bobby, TJ is like you," John said, as if he needed to remind the man of that. "What does it matter if he saw you?"

Bobby said nothing, and John thought he knew.

It was because Bobby had run away. He'd abandoned his peers at FUCN'A and left them all to work for Bazyli, in hopes of a cure. If TJ saw him wandering around, he'd report it.

In the silence that seemed to have all the answers, Matthew shoved Bobby off him. "Where's Bazyli?" He looked at Rachel. "Is he back yet?"

"He's not here." Rachel shook her head, looking at her brother, then TJ, and then at John. "His car is gone. I don't... I don't know where he is."

This was a lot of new people. John could only imagine what was going through her head.

"Is he *ever* around?" Gerard muttered.

Matthew glared at him.

"Does he need to be tied up?" John asked, trying to remember what TJ was like. He hadn't spoken to the man, ever, really. Not while they overlapped at FUCN'A.

TJ had been a victim of a madwoman's experiments.

John was the criminal who'd helped her.

But back in the labs... John tried to remember. He thought he'd recalled TJ being quiet in his glass cage. Before John had been elevated to henchman status, he'd been in a cage close to TJ's. John had tried to talk to him a time or two, but he never got an answer.

TJ had absolutely refused to look at his own reflection in the glass. Seemed harmless and kind of sad.

"He attacked me!" Bobby snarled.

"You look fine to me," John shot back. "Don't be such a pussy."

Bobby's mandibles fluttered. He got right into John's space. "Shay that shit again," he challenged, spittle flying, the long, coarse hairs around his mouth twitching.

John was itchy just standing there next to him.

John felt his inner cobra coming forward. Answering that challenge. Wanting to fight.

He held back.

He hadn't been given a dose of the blockers in a while, and he didn't want to go around reminding people that he could shift if they didn't need to know.

Bobby's eyes crinkled in a wicked, strange smile. Those mandibles twitched again, a drop of something that could be drool, or venom, forming at the tip of one of his fangs.

"Yeah, that's right." His voice was less slurred now that he thought he had control, taking John's lack of fight to mean surrender. "I looked up how spiders and snakes fight in the wild. The spider *always* wins."

Cocksucker.

"So what are you going to do with him?" John asked, pointing at TJ.

"Bring him to the fox," Gerard said. "This guy used to look like us. He was fixed. Maybe his blood will—"

"You don't need his blood," Matthew snapped, a vein pulsing at the side of his neck. "John's already volunteered. We're using his."

"John came out normal." Bobby rounded on Matthew,

pointing a finger at his own, spidery face. "He never looked like this. TJ did. They fixed him, and they didn't fix me!"

"My flowers will help," Rachel said. "They're almost ready. I've got some powder ready for when he comes back."

"He's not going to figure it out with some dumb flowers," Bobby snapped, his eyes wild. "Don't you get it? The flowers are just a way to keep you busy. I'm sick of all this blind hope that Bazyli is going to do *anything*. I'm tired of looking like a fucking freak!"

"Maybe you should have stuck it out with FUC then," John said, shocking himself with his lack of sympathy for the guy.

Bobby looked at him, a fire in his eyes.

John shrugged. "I've only been here for a short time. Just saying that you might've already got the same treatment TJ did if you hadn't thrown your hat in with the fox."

Bobby roared, flying at him.

John quickly ducked to the side, sticking his foot out and tripping up Bobby's legs.

The man recovered shockingly well. He wasn't nearly as clumsy as he looked, grabbing John around the waist, lifting him up high, and then bringing him down with all the power of gravity.

The wind completely went out of John's sails. Even he couldn't believe the hidden strength Bobby seemed to possess.

Or the wild, red rage he saw in the man's eyes as his hands came around John's throat.

"This is because of you!" he roared, his spittle and venom catching John on his face. "You and that fucking bitch!"

John closed his lips. He didn't know how poisonous

Bobby was, but he wasn't taking the risk that his venom would affect him.

Bobby squeezed. John couldn't breathe. He couldn't kick the man off him either.

Distantly, he saw Rachel rush forward.

No. No! Don't get in the middle of a fight!

She wasn't alone. Matthew was with her. Gerard stood back, as useless and cowardly as ever, wringing his hands and practically pissing himself while Rachel and Matthew tried to drag Bobby off him.

"I'll kill you! I'll fucking kill you!"

He just might. John's face suddenly felt hot. Darkness began to consume his vision. He was looking through a tunnel the width of a straw.

He scrambled for the plastic knife he'd kept hidden on him, slashing it out across the man's face.

Bobby roared, flying backward, blood dropping from his mandibles, releasing John's throat in the chaos.

John sucked in a heavy breath. With Matthew and Rachel yanking Bobby back, he managed to roll to the side, out from under Bobby's weight.

Considering he'd only used a little plastic knife, there was a shocking amount of blood.

Matthew punched Bobby in the face, sending him flying backward.

"Don't you ever do that again!" Matthew roared, closing in on the man in an impressive show of anger. "You hear me? *Ever* again!"

There was no way a rage like that was for John.

He looked up, heart sinking when he saw just what had Matthew so up in arms about.

Rachel sat on her knees, holding her left arm limply in her other hand, a dazed expression on her face.

He didn't see a large amount of blood on her arm, but that wasn't what had John's heart hammering.

No. No.

He scrambled to her side. "Let me see. Let me see."

She looked at him, and as though in a dream or a daze, she did show him.

A scratch. That was it, but already a strange yellow-and-green side effect was taking place in her skin.

It hadn't come from his little knife. He didn't accidentally get her when he'd sliced at Bobby.

But he wished he had, because the alternative was worse.

The venom from Bobby's fangs. He must have scratched her when he threw his head back

Calm. John had to keep calm.

"Okay, all right. We can deal with this." John didn't have a belt, but he could see Gerard did. John rushed to him, grabbing at his pants.

Gerard yanked himself back, outrage on his face. "What are you—?"

"I need a belt!" He yanked it off the man's waist, ignoring Gerard's outrage and confusion.

The guy didn't seem all there right now. John didn't blame him for not being able to keep his head clear, but he needed people who wouldn't stand around like idiots when shit hit the fan.

He rushed back to Rachel. "Okay, this is going to be tight on your arm."

She nodded, seeming to understand exactly what he was doing and why, allowing him to wrap her forearm with the belt as he tied it tight enough to cut off any further circulation.

Meanwhile, Matthew and Bobby screamed at each other.

"It washn't my fault! She grabbed me!"

"I don't care, you idiot! Have some goddamn self-control!"

John glanced back, watching as Matthew, holding tightly to Bobby's collar, slammed him into the concrete ground.

His eyes were red, and there was blood on Bobby's chest and on Matthew's talons.

John wished it was him. Wished he was the one who could beat the shit out of Bobby for what he'd done. He had this to take care of instead.

"Do you know what sort of venom Bobby has?" It occurred to John that he had no idea. "Is he actually venomous?"

It might not be anything dangerous at all. Not all shifters retained all the features of the animals they could transform into.

Rachel, to John's terror, nodded. "Dad said it could be bad."

Fuck.

"How bad?"

She seemed so far away. She seemed like she was getting ready to spiral into a panic. He snapped his fingers in front of her face, making her blink and look at him.

"Rachel, stay here with me. Is it bad?"

"I... I don't...I don't know."

He nodded. That wasn't good.

"Okay, if your dad didn't tell you how bad it was when he tested Bobby, then it can't be that bad, right?"

That seemed to be the right thing to say. Rachel heaved a sigh. "Right. It... it burns though. Not in the good way, either."

He didn't understand. "The good way?"

"Guys?" Gerard called.

Rachel wet her lips. "Like, when you kissed me." She smiled, blushing a little. "That was a good burning."

"Hey, guys?"

The fact that she could smile and joke, even as sweat beaded on her forehead, had to be a good thing. John was going to take it as a good omen and nothing else.

"Guys!"

"What?" John snapped, rising to his feet, rounding on the man who he partially blamed for this whole thing.

He and Bobby were close, often egging each other on and encouraging their shared misery. Gerard's tentacle fingers wiggled, making a wet, slippery noise as he pointed, using his whole arm, since his fingers couldn't hold much of a point, to the truck.

"He's gone."

"What?" Matthew shot himself off of Bobby. He looked down at his sister then at the truck, torn between the two.

Gerard was right. TJ was nowhere to be found.

16

TJ needed to get the fuck out of there, but the way he'd come in was not going to fly.

He'd been a cadet for barely two weeks, and already he was in massive shit.

And Matthew was involved.

What the fuck?

Running through the damp, cement corridors with the many pipes overhead and flickering lights was giving him all kinds of déjà vu, shooting him back to a time when he was a test subject, in a place just like this.

Only with more people on staff. These halls here were shockingly empty.

He looked through the windows of any door he could find. More empty labs. More vacant rooms.

Some with a few beds. A few empty tanks. Some tables with straps on them, cabinets opened, bottles and clip-boards, and...

He shivered. He couldn't look at those.

He wasn't about to let himself be put on a table again.

No fucking way.

Luckily, freeing himself from zip ties wasn't his only talent.

After he'd enrolled as a cadet, one of the FUC agents actually taught him how to pick a lock. Useful if he ever found himself in handcuffs or locked up by the bad guys. Or stuck in the situation he was in now.

And Bobby and the tentacle guy hadn't exactly been thorough when they'd searched him. They took the phone and wallet from his pocket, which wasn't good.

But his kit had been in a holster at his ankle.

And by kit, he meant a small leather case that held three needle-like tools that could help him pop open a basic lock or filing cabinet. He wouldn't be taking over the world with it, but it made him feel like he had a little advantage.

But he didn't have a great deal of time. It was just a matter of time before they discovered that he was gone.

One minute. Maybe two.

He needed to move fast.

He needed to find a door out, and he got the feeling, the farther he ran, that he was just rushing deeper into the compound.

If he remembered anything about these places, there was usually a back door. An emergency escape if the authorities showed up. He might come across it if he was lucky, but the main office would have the location for sure.

The main baddies always had to have a direct escape route.

He had to find it.

"Where the hell is he?"

"Find him!"

Fuck.

"You idiots take Rachel to the infirmary!" Matthew's voice. "I'll hunt him down."

TJ swallowed over the lump in his throat at Matthew's choice of words.

Fuck. To think that TJ had just started to feel good about things. About his fixed face, about a blossoming friendship —maybe even more—with the mysterious Matthew.

Just to discover that he'd been hoodwinked, tricked by the very same kind of people who'd experimented on him in the first place.

He kept going, becoming desperate, feeling his panic starting to rise with every passing second. He started searching for doors that were unlocked, opening them wide whenever he could.

If he could trick Matthew into thinking he'd gone in, make the guy waste his time looking under desks and in closets, then all the better.

Another trick he'd picked up in his short time as a cadet.

God. He'd been so stupid, trusting a man he'd just met.

Then, finally, *finally*, he found it.

Or, he thought he had.

There was no window at this door, but he didn't think it was a closet holding cleaning supplies.

This door was locked, and it was in a corridor with old lockers where the staff would keep their shit while they went to experiment on the people they'd either tricked or kidnapped.

In the distance, TJ heard doors slamming.

"TJ! Come on. I know you're there. We can talk."

"Fuck you," TJ muttered to himself.

He'd been *nice* to the asshole. He hadn't laughed at him when the guy didn't know the answer to, Who was the author who wrote: *How The Grinch Stole Christmas*.

Matt had seemed embarrassed, but TJ hadn't judged him. It was easy to be strange in the town they lived in. With the FUC Academy right there, and the facility being used to house freed experiments, such as himself, for months, TJ was used to being around unusual folks.

He pushed the thoughts out of his mind and focused. He had the door unlocked after the longest four seconds of his life.

TJ pushed his way inside, quietly closed it behind him, and locked it again.

He stayed quiet. He had no idea how strong an owl beast's scenting was, but he prayed the guy wouldn't sniff him out where he was.

He could hear Matt rushing down the hall. His breath caught when the door handle in front of him jiggled. There seemed to be hesitation. TJ couldn't breathe.

Then, finally, Matt walked away. TJ could hear his shoes as he rushed down the hall, likely checking more doors.

Christ, TJ's heart was beating so fast. Blood rushed to his ears, making them ring.

No. He had to breathe. He had to keep his calm. Another lesson he'd learned.

If he let himself panic, he wouldn't manage to help anyone, let alone himself.

His mind rushed back to the drinks he and Matt had shared. Matt had been oddly quiet about his home life. His age. Almost everything, really.

All TJ had been able to get out of him was that he had a sister and a dad and he cared for both of them very much.

That was it.

The way he carried himself suggested there was a lot more to Matt's story, and TJ had even suspected he was another experiment. Maybe from a different compound than the one TJ came from.

Another poor bastard the world had turned on its head for, who suddenly had to navigate life for what it really was.

TJ knew what that felt like. He'd felt for the man. So getting his number, being able to text him after their drink, trying to make plans to meet up again had felt...

Good.

TJ had wanted to help him.

He was such a stupid fucking asshole.

TJ was in no position to help anyone with anything. He had almost no training. He was...

Stop. Pity party later. He had to think about how he was going to get out of there.

He glanced back, and, yes, it was an office, but unlike the others he'd passed by, this one wasn't empty. There was a desk, but it had personal items sitting on it. Papers with actual notes on them, a laptop, pens, and, interestingly enough, a fidget spinner.

Cool. He was taking that, because fuck this guy.

TJ stuck the toy in his pocket, hoping it would annoy the fuck out of whoever used this office.

There was a small picture frame on the desk.

He looked at it.

A man with silver hair, wearing a grey suit and white gloves. The only thing he was missing was a cane and a monocle. Maybe a villainous mustache. He looked like someone who might be in charge around there.

The other notable thing about the photo, aside from how the man was dressed, was the two people with him.

Matt was one of them, standing stiffly next to the silver-haired man. The other person was the woman he'd seen in the garage. The woman with thick red hair. She stood more happily on the other side of the white-haired man. The man's gloved hand held her shoulder. She leaned in close, smiling for the camera.

She wore the same green dress and black flats.

This man had to be Matt's father. The woman, his sister. It was interesting information, but it wasn't getting him out of here.

TJ started pulling open all the drawers in the desk, tanking them back. There was very little to be found inside. A calculator. More pens and pencils.

A crappy child's drawing with a very off-looking heart on it. The words *I love you Daddy* scrawled in a child's writing in crayon. Two stick figures on it. One clearly a little girl, from the triangle skirt that smaller stick figure wore. The other a taller man with silver hair.

It couldn't be Matt's red-haired sister though. This little girl also had silver hair.

She'd used the glittery silver crayon. TJ could see the shimmer.

The paper looked old, folded and unfolded many times over.

There were dried splotches on it, dotted here and there. He didn't want to think about what that could be. Did Matt and his sister have another sibling? Someone who'd died?

Oh well, not relevant to TJ's escape.

He abandoned the desk and started looking around the walls, figuring the asshole would have a door hidden behind one of the filing cabinets or bookshelves.

Bingo.

He found a door behind a cabinet, pulling out his tools to unlock the door.

He got it open and...

Immediately shut it again.

What the fuck?

No way. What he'd just seen couldn't be real.

He took a breath and steadied himself. He was slower this time, opening the door and letting the pink glow from inside wash over him.

A tank. Filled with liquid being illuminated by pink bulbs hanging above it. There was a machine attached to the tank that whirled as it pumped something into the water.

And floating in the water?

What looked like... *holy shit.* It was a fucking baby.

He looked at it, really looked, walking closer until he could reach out and tap the glass. Was the thing inside alive? He was pretty sure it was. It had an umbilical cord and everything.

It didn't look totally developed, though. He wasn't an expert on fetal sizes, but he could conclude that it didn't look ready to be "born" yet.

So tiny.

All thoughts of escape left his mind as he *had* to figure out what was going on here. He'd seen plenty of results of shifter experiments... but they'd all gone in as fully formed people. He'd never seen anything like *this*.

FUC will want to know about this.

There were small glass jars next to the tank. Some sort of pink powder inside. A few dried leaves. TJ dug around, finding papers and notes.

He read the first page, which were notes from a Mr. Bazyli Smith

Interesting name.

It was the rest that caught his attention.

Subject Number Thirteen: Rachel.

Number thirteen? "What the hell?"

"What are you doing here?"

TJ whirled around, backing hard into the wall as he stared at Matt, who stood there in the open office door, his enormously tall body taking up almost the entire doorway.

And what appeared to be a spare key in his hand.

"Stay away from me," TJ said.

Matt pressed his lips together then shut the door quietly before facing him. "I won't hurt you, but you can't be in here."

"I agree, so tell me how to get out of here and I'll go."

Matt's sorry expression wasn't what TJ had hoped for. "You know I... I can't."

TJ was so fucking furious. He wished he could fight the man, but he wasn't that sort of shifter. Hell, even if he'd been a tiger, their size difference alone would mean he stood no chance.

"I thought you were..." TJ sighed. "I thought you needed help."

"What were you doing sneaking around? Getting caught by those two bozos?" To his credit, Matt did look sorry.

"Nothing," TJ snapped. "I wasn't sneaking around. I was hiking through the damn woods. I was literally minding my own business when I saw Bobby and his idiot friend fighting on the side of the road, and I stupidly stopped and offered help."

Matt looked confused. "Bobby and Gerard were fighting?"

TJ eyed Matt, realizing he didn't know what those two had been doing out there.

"I'd overheard them talking about how they were thinking of going to FUC, letting them know you're all here and what you're doing. Guess they got tired of waiting for a cure."

"Because FUC is so quick to help other people?" Matt

snapped, his shoulders going tight. "They would have let my sister die."

TJ could understand the emotional connection and why someone like Matt would believe that this was the only way to save someone, but there was more going on than a cure for some illness.

"What is all this?" TJ asked, pointing to the tank with the floating fetus.

"What?" Matt jerked back, seeming to look at the tank for the first time.

"Rachel. Subject thirteen." TJ pointed to the notes he held. He held out the papers for Matt, who snatched them and immediately began flipping through them.

"No, Rachel is my sister. The red-haired woman you saw in the garage."

The expression on Matt's face told TJ that this was news to him as well.

Maybe TJ had been right about him the first time.

Ever since his shifting ability had been fixed, TJ's sense of smell had vastly improved. He didn't need it to know that Matt was having something of a crisis at the moment.

"This... this can't... This isn't possible." Matt looked back at the tank, as though he needed to confirm for himself what he was reading.

Then Matt looked at him with such helplessness in his eyes that TJ forgot all about his previous anger. Hell, it suddenly didn't matter how he'd gotten to this point in the first place.

"Does she know?"

Matt's mouth opened and closed several times. Nothing came out. He had to shake his head.

A horrible thought occurred to TJ just then. "What about you?"

Matt's gaze, suddenly more alert, jerked to him. "What about me?"

TJ pointed to the tank. "Are you... Was this how you..."

"No." Matt shook his head, a small vein pulsing at the side of his neck. His forehead suddenly having a bright shine to it, sweat building.

"No, that's not... that's not possible. He would have... My dad would have said something."

TJ didn't say anything. The kindest thing for him in that moment seemed to be to just let this information wash over Matt, to let him process it. Matt's breathing seemed to quicken. He looked back at the tank where the machine was plugged in, slowly humming and gurgling.

He glanced away quickly, rubbing his hand down his face.

TJ shouldn't.

He did.

He reached out, laying his hand on the guy's shoulder.

"I don't know what exactly is going on," he said, trying to be calm as Matt stared at him with wild eyes. "But I know what it's like to have something heavy dropped on you. Maybe not exactly like this, but..."

He was probably being stupid. How the hell was he ever supposed to relate to something like this? To the realization that the person you thought was your father was actually growing shifters. Not just experimenting on existing people and shifters... but... possibly *cloning...*

TJ was just the guy whose face and body got fucked up from experiments. *This* was a whole other level of fucked up.

"I need to get to my sister," Matt said, dropping the notes onto a table. "Bobby bit her.

"He's venomous," TJ said, remembering what he knew

from their days at the lab and at FUCN'A. "But don't worry. I don't think he's that deadly."

"You knew Bobby?" Matt grabbed his shoulders. His fingers dug in tight enough that he was going to leave bruises. "Are you sure? Will she be okay?"

That was the thing. TJ *didn't* know Bobby. Not that well, anyway, and what little he did know of the guy...

Well, TJ had done some shit when he was desperate for a cure, but Bobby's inclination toward being a massive prick went beyond a normal lashing out.

He tried to remember more from the time they'd both spent at the FUC Academy. There hadn't been much gossip, but...

"She's going to need medicine. And time in a hospital. It shouldn't kill her, but I don't know what will happen if she's not treated."

Matt's nostrils flared. "Are you sure?"

"They let him in the cafeteria with us all the time. No one liked the sight of his... face"—the spider fangs and the hair had been so uncomfortable, even to TJ, who had been the ugliest one of the bunch of them—"so the FUC agents and doctors couldn't have been so worried there would be accidents."

"I don't think I can take her to a doctor," Matt said, his face dropping.

TJ was sure that was their best bet, but he wasn't sure he could convince Matt to take her. "Do you have the resources here? For venom?"

Matt's hesitation was answer enough.

He didn't know. Or he didn't trust the materials they had.

"Matt, come with me. FUC will take you in."

Matt shook his head.

TJ had to keep trying. "You're not a criminal. That man,

your dad, Bazyli, whatever his name is, he tricked you and your sister. You need to get out of here."

Matt kept shaking his head. "They'll kill her. Me too. FUC will kill us for existing."

"That's insane," TJ said, shocked. "It's completely false information. If that were true, why didn't they kill me or Bobby or John?"

The words hit Matt and seemed to sink into his skull as he processed the logic for the first time. He continued to shake his head, though TJ wasn't sure if he was refusing to accept the truth or just in shock over the fact that he'd been tricked for so long.

TJ grabbed his shoulders.

Matt jerked.

"She can't stay here. She could very well die if she sits here waiting for help. And I *promise* you that FUC won't kill her. Or you."

Matt's Adam's apple worked in a hard swallow. TJ could hear the drumming of his heart, could almost feel the pulse of blood from under his shirt and skin.

Then, to TJ's immense relief, Matt gave in.

"Okay."

17

"Sit right here." To John's own ears, he sounded calm and collected. "There you go. Good. Bobby, I need to talk to you. Gerard, get her some water to drink. And something to clean out the scratch. Lots of it."

Inside, he was flying off the handle.

Rachel looked pale. More so than usual, which was saying something, considering she spent most of her time underground.

Bobby, with a swelling cheek from where Matthew had punched him, had the good sense to not fight John when he grabbed the man by the upper arm and pulled him just far enough away from Rachel so they could talk.

"Don't bullshit me. How venomous are you?"

"I don't know."

"Fuck you, you don't know."

"I don't!" Bobby snapped, the both of them quieting down as he glanced back at her.

"The boss took a shample, so did the docs at FUC, but I never found out. No one told me."

Don't freak out. This could be handled.

"Okay, maybe it's not that bad. What happens when tarantulas bite people in the wild?"

"Depends on the spider," Bobby said, sounding calmer, looking at Rachel with an oddly detached expression. "For some people, their flesh rots away and has to be—"

"Okay, stop. I don't want Rachel hearing you say that." And in truth, he didn't want to hear it either. It sounded horrible and gruesome.

And despite the medicine Rachel's father worked on, he had no clue if this run-down place had the tools needed to treat her.

There was one place that definitely would, though.

"We have to get her out of here."

"What? Where?" Bobby demanded.

John looked at him.

Bobby shook his head. "No! No fucking way! Her old man would kill us all."

"If she dies here because of your venom, then you're dead anyway."

John turned back to Gerard and Rachel.

Her skin was turning clammy and grey. Gerard, to his credit, was doing a good job of tenderly wiping down her cut, cleaning it with alcohol, but it was obvious whatever venom Bobby carried around in his body had made it into her system already.

"Always said I wanted to spend more time up above." Rachel tried smiling at him, but it looked more like a grimace than anything else. Then her eyes turned sad. "What if they hurt me?"

"They won't," John said, immediately grabbing her hands.

They felt clammy.

Cold.

She was trembling.

"I swear they won't. That's not what they do."

Bobby snorted.

John wanted to punch him.

"Please trust me, at least on this. They're not going to hurt you. They'll want to help you."

"What about Matthew?"

John took a breath. "I'll take you, and if it's just you and me, I won't tell anyone where this place is."

Rachel frowned. "You won't?"

"No, never." John shook his head.

What was there to tell? That a fox shifter had his daughter growing and drying out flowers and was harboring Bobby and Gerard? John had been there long enough that he hadn't seen any other prisoners aside from himself. The place wasn't loaded with hundreds of vulnerable kids and adults who'd been tricked into signing their lives away.

It was something else.

"They'll chain her to a bed and grill her until she tells them about this place," Bobby said. "They'll lock you up, too. You're more a monster than me."

That was true. His face ached at the idea of being attacked by the owl again.

If John did this, there was a good chance it might be a long time before he saw Rachel again—if ever.

But it didn't matter. She needed medical attention, and John had long ago resigned himself to whatever punishment life doled out to him.

"Gerard, finish wrapping her arm. We're leaving."

"You're not allowed to!" Bobby snapped.

"Fuck you." John's opinion about the fox was up in the air, but he still hadn't forgiven Bobby for putting that bag over his head and helping to kidnap him.

Gerard quickly wiped some cream across Rachel's arm before wrapping it up tight. The belt was still in place on her upper forearm, but there was no knowing how long that would do the trick.

John pulled Rachel into his arms. She weighed almost nothing.

This was his fault.

He wanted to fucking kill Bobby.

"You can't just fucking leave!" Bobby snapped.

John was already moving toward the door as Bobby continued to shout. "FUC will come back here and shut everything down!"

"We were on our way to talk to FUC agents when you found that guy," Gerard said.

John stopped. He turned and looked at Bobby. Even Rachel managed to summon the energy to hold up her head.

"Really?"

"No!" Bobby snapped.

Gerard did something shocking.

He extended his arm, truck keys dangling from his tentacles.

"Seriously?" John asked.

"Just take me with you," he said. "Fuck this place. I want someone to *fix* me. Bobby and I were going to turn the fox in. We thought the information on this place would shoot us to the top of the waiting list of people who got treatment."

Christ, that sounded morbid. But John wasn't in any kind of position to judge. He'd done plenty to try to save himself in the past.

"You motherfucker!" Bobby roared. "You spineless sack of shit!"

John ignored him, jerking his head for Gerard to follow. "Let's go."

"You're not fucking leaving!"

Bobby grabbed John by the shoulder, whirling him around.

It was Rachel who acted.

She threw her arm out, claws out, slapping Bobby across the face, leaving marks across his hairy, tarantula cheek where she got him.

Bobby stared at her, shocked.

John was stunned, too.

Rachel smiled. "That was worth the itchy hand."

Bobby's stunned silence lasted for one more second. His gaze cast down to the little remote hanging around Rachel's neck.

He lunged for it.

Gerard stepped in his way, grabbing Bobby's shoulders and pushing him back as John ducked out of the way.

"Go!"

John didn't have to be told twice.

He ran.

He ran like Rachel's life depended on it.

He made it back to the garage, which looked brighter than it had the last time he'd been there.

Namely, because the garage door was wide open and the fox shifter's car had pulled in.

He must have just arrived because he had just killed his engine and was stepping out of the car.

His suit was more rumpled now compared to how John was used to seeing it, as though he'd been running around, trying to get several tasks finished. There were boxes in the back seat of his car. John couldn't tell what they were, but he figured if was what the fox had been out collecting.

"What is this?" the fox asked.

John didn't need this right now, but if he was her father, and if he did love her, he'd help.

"Bobby poisoned her. There was a fight. We need to get her some help."

"Show me," the fox demanded, storming toward them both, his eyes fixed on John, as though he'd been the one to do this.

His gaze softened on Rachel, however, taking her cheeks into his gloved hands.

"Daddy?" Rachel asked, as if she couldn't see him. "I'm hot."

This was bad. She was reacting too fast. The venom was pushing through her system too quickly.

"Yes, sweet. I'm here." The fox shifter took a deep breath. "Daddy is here."

"Sir, she needs a hospital," John said, realizing that with her father accompanying them, they could get help outside FUCN'A.

"Yes," said the fox, sounding detached. "She cannot stay here."

Still, he didn't move back to his car. He stared at his daughter.

Rachel's head lolled. She was burning up and sweating.

The fox kept staring at her.

"Sir!" John had no patience for this. "We need to go now."

"I smell someone else here," he said. "Who else is here?"

"No one. We need to leave."

The fox took a step back from them. Away from his poisoned daughter.

What the fuck?

"Sir? She needs help." John was having a hard time controlling his tone.

"Do you have the keys to the truck?"

"Yes."

"Then drive her. I'm needed here."

John jerked back. "*What?*"

The dead-eyed stare on the fox's face suddenly vanished, replaced with something biting and acidic.

"Drive her to the hospital or to FUCN'A or wherever you want. You can report to them what you will. I am needed here." He pressed the button on his car keychain, which made his vehicle lock, the lights flashing.

Then he marched toward the doors leading into the facility.

"This is your daughter!" Disgust, so filthy and wretched it was vile to contain it, rose up inside John's body. "She needs you! Don't you fucking care?"

"Be quick. She needs medical attention." The fox stopped, gloved hand resting on the doorway. He barely glanced back at them. "Take care of her."

Then he was gone, out of sight as quickly as though he were being chased.

"D-daddy?" Rachel asked.

John hated him. He hated that motherfucker more than anyone he'd ever encountered.

He ran for the truck, forced to buckle Rachel into the passenger seat, to not hold her in his arms as he started the engine.

The garage door was still wide open. The sun, which he hadn't seen in weeks, poured through.

It was dangerous to drive like this. He was blinded for too many seconds when he drove out, but thankfully, his eyes adjusted, and it was a short trip down a bumpy, unpaved road before he knew exactly where he was.

Closer to FUCN'A than any town big enough for a clinic or hospital.

There was only one choice. All signs pointed right where he needed to go.

FUC would lock him up, but they'd treat Rachel right. They'd save her, and they'd rehabilitate her. Just as they did for all the others. Just like they did for Charlie.

"M-Matthew? Where's Matthew? W-where's Daddy?"

John clenched his hands around the steering wheel as he turned on the next backroad that would lead them to FUC. He remembered how he'd been conned into loving someone who'd been using him. How he'd been made to feel sorry for that madwoman.

Hell, there was a time when he wanted that woman to be his mother. His family.

The difference was he knew she was crazy. Knew she wasn't actually his mother from the beginning. Knew that if she'd kept that baby she'd stolen, that kid would grow up not knowing.

Was that what had happened to Rachel?

He was definitely zooming down the road, way past the speed limit, pushing the truck to its limit.

He knew where it was. He knew where everything was.

What would he tell them when they arrived? He still didn't know if that dirty fox was actually Rachel's kin or not. Or Matthew's. The man had looked like he cared... until he didn't. What man turned his back on his kid? What sort of parent would trust someone like John with their daughter?

The gate to the facility came into view. A car was just being let through the security gate when John saw it.

Knowing it was his best shot of getting her there, he floored it, zooming through the open gate right after the first car.

He veered off the road, driving over the grass to pass the car ahead of him. In his rearview mirror, he saw both the driver as well as the security guard shaking their fists at him.

"We're here. We're here," John reassured Rachel as he got back on the road and drove around the main building—WANC, as they called it—to the side with the med wing.

He left the cab and ran over to the passenger side, opening the door and pulling Rachel into his arms, oblivious to the security personnel who'd gathered.

"John," she said, her voice soft. "Thank you, John."

At least she knew she was with him. At least she wasn't scared.

"I got you. I swear."

FUC was going to lock him away for the rest of his life. He might never see her again.

Didn't matter.

He didn't care.

He needed to save her. He needed her to live.

He looked around at all the agents who surrounded them. "*Help!* Someone help. She's been poisoned!"

18

Bazyli rushed to his office, a surge of horror striking him to see the door wide open.

No one was inside.

It didn't matter.

His secret room was open.

No.

God, no.

He rushed to the tank, nearly losing all the strength in his knees from the relief of seeing it still plugged in and still operational.

His daughter was still alive inside.

She was still there.

He had to get them out of here.

That snake would be taking Rachel Number Four to the hospital. He would tell them where she had been found.

He needed to get Number Thirteen out of here.

There was a backup battery. Four of them should the generator for the facility finally give out. They were already attached to the tank, built into the portable cart system that he'd designed. He simply needed to unplug it from the main power source. It would last for days until he could get to another facility.

"Gerard! Bobby!"

He wanted to kill Bobby in particular. This was because of him.

He wheeled out the tank and its life support, glancing at his desk to see Rachel's drawing laying on it. Not where he left it but, thankfully, unharmed. He grabbed it, folded it, and tucked it into his pocket. After some debate, he did the same with the photo on his desk.

But he couldn't leave just yet.

"I'll be right back, baby girl." Baz left the tank and rushed from his office. He needed more petals. More powder. And more seeds. He could not leave without them.

Those flowers had been perfect. Cultivated and genetically modified to contain the exact materials he needed for his children.

"Matthew!"

The boy did not answer him.

No answer from him, Bobby, or Gerard. Plus, that odd scent of someone unfamiliar in the compound. Not good. He'd been gone only a few hours and this happened. Unbelievable. It was no longer safe here.

On his way to the grow room, he understood a little more.

Gerard's body, bloody around the neck and hands, lay against the wall, the result of a gruesome fight. One of his tentacled fingers had been bitten off.

But he wasn't dead. Gerard blinked slowly. "Sir?"

Baz was shocked he was alive at all, but Gerard wasn't his concern. He stepped around him.

He needed those flowers.

In the grow room, Baz collected what he needed. It

looked as though Number Four had recently put some petals and leaves to be dried in the machine.

Good girl.

She had always been a good girl. Even if she was the wrong girl, she had been good.

That worthless snake had better take care of her.

Baz returned to the hallway, rushing back toward his office.

"Sir?" Gerard called again weakly. Baz quickly side-stepped him again. He would be dead soon enough, Baz needed to get back to the garage.

He collected all he could before he rolled the tank system out to the garage.

He had to disassemble it to place the tank on the passenger's seat and run the life support lines from the back seats to it.

Once everything was in place, he got into the driver's seat, lovingly stroking the tank. "It's all right, sweetheart. Daddy's here."

He started the engine and pulled out of the garage for the last time.

On his dashboard, he pulled up the EXIT commands for the compound. The gasoline that had been stored for the power generators was released through the fire sprinklers when he tapped the correct command on the touch screen.

In the kitchens, and the labs, a few electronics that were plugged in would begin the process of overheating and sparking.

Igniting.

He saw the glow in the distance behind him through his rearview mirror, and he kept right on going.

To the next safe house.

19

Rachel felt hot and swollen and sweaty and all sorts of terrible. She couldn't remember ever feeling like this before.

But then, a man in a white lab coat was there. He held a clipboard. His voice sounded so very far away, but Rachel found herself relaxing just a little.

Her father wasn't there. He had left her.

"Where is John?" she managed to ask.

"Will she be all right? Is she going to live?"

There he was.

The thing that had been twisting and writhing uncomfortably in her stomach settled.

"She'll be fine," someone replied. A man who was not her father.

What about Matthew? Where was her brother? Did FUC have him? Had they been found?

"You're all right. I promise." She recognized John's voice and his touch as he reached out and clasped her hand.

She settled down again.

John was there. That was something.

She felt good, warm, and safe. Much warmer than she ever had in the compound.

That feeling, along with John's hand in her own, allowed her to slip away again.

When she opened her eyes again, it felt like she'd been sleeping for so long. Her eyes were swollen. Her throat was dry, and that comforting warmth and weight of John's hand in hers was nowhere to be found.

There was someone else there, though.

Someone not wearing a white coat.

Her vision was clearer, though her body felt heavy.

The man was tall. He looked like he hadn't slept in a while. He had bags under his eyes.

He had dark brown hair with reading glasses perched on his nose. He seemed lost in a file in his hands.

He looked a little like Matthew.

She frowned, blinking several times just to make sure that it wasn't Matthew there after all.

"Hello?"

"Oh!" The man took his reading glasses off. "Hello."

She frowned, tried to sit up, then winced.

"Try not to move. Your bandages were just changed."

"What?" Rachel looked down at herself, needing to see, and then nearly freaked out at the sight of the enormous cast hiding her arm.

Her arm felt swollen and hot and weird, tingly at the tips of her fingers and then numb everywhere else.

Panic rose up in her chest.

"Wh-where's John?" She looked up at the man. "Where is he? Where am I?"

"You're at the Furry United Coalition Newbie Academy. In the hospital wing, to be exact." He came closer, turning that clipboard he'd been looking at. "This is you, correct?"

He lifted some of the pages so she could see...

Herself. That was a picture of herself. With Matthew.

In one of the dumpsters outside of the FUCNA Academy. She had no doubt he probably had more photos, but that was enough for her to know that she was caught.

The thief had been apprehended.

She'd thought they had painted any cameras that could see them. She'd been wrong.

Rachel swallowed hard. "Where's John?" He brought her here, but he said they wouldn't hurt her. She'd believed him.

But these were the people they'd been hiding from. The ones who would want to take her shifting abilities from her.

Who would want to hurt her.

Who were probably hurting John.

"He's fine."

"He was just trying to help me."

"I know. He brought you in," the man explained. "My name is Albert, by the way. I promise, no one is here to hurt you."

"Albert?"

He nodded, holding out his hand.

Very slowly, because it seemed rude not to, Rachel reached out with her good hand to take his, shaking it.

Where had she heard that name before?

"Are... are you the man whose baby John stole?"

"He told you about that?" The man looked surprised.

Rachel yanked her hand back, a chill rising up her spine. This was the man that put those scars on John's face.

"I... He told me." She couldn't look away from his hands. She didn't see any claws, but that didn't mean he wasn't about to bring them out. Was he going to do the same to her as he'd done to John?

"I won't hurt you." Albert frowned, glancing down at his fingers where she stared.

She didn't believe him. "Where is John?" she asked again, wanting to know if he was even in the same building as her anymore.

Albert seemed to debate with himself whether or not he should answer her.

He seemed to decide on *not.* "Who is the man in the photo with you?"

She glared at him. She was not about to answer that.

"Please tell me," Albert asked again. "It's important."

"I want to see John before I cooperate with anything," she demanded. Red hairs began pushing through the pores of her skin. Her tiny claws formed at her fingertips. "Did you hurt him? Again?"

She wanted to stand up to her full height. She wanted to threaten him. Wanted to fight him. Matthew had once said she looked adorable when she was trying to be threatening. From the expression on Albert's face, he thought the same thing.

Which annoyed her.

"John is a criminal.'"

"He's not!" And she would be damned if she let this man call him that.

"I just told you—"

"He tried to make it right. He gave your baby back! He didn't *want* to hurt anyone. He was being used by the wrong people, and he had no other choice."

Albert frowned, not looking remotely convinced. Perhaps, after what he and his wife had gone through, it would take more than one angry red-haired woman to convince him.

"Please let me see him," she begged, forcing herself to calm down and stop her shift. "Where is he?"

She needed to see him. More than she needed to see her father or even Matthew. And that was such a strange realization.

John brought her here. He walked right into danger to save her life. Who was going to fight for him?

No one.

But her.

"Maybe I can make something happen," Albert said, clearing his throat awkwardly. "But you can't talk to him right now even if I took you to him. John's been in his cobra form for a while."

She blinked. "He... he has?"

It occurred to her that she'd never seen him in his other shape.

"He answered our questions, made sure you were getting the care you needed, and has been in his snake form ever since." Albert reached to the side. He grabbed something off a shelf. She hadn't noticed it before, but when he held it out to her, her breath caught.

The shock collar and her remote.

She reached up to her neck, realizing someone must have removed the shoelace and remote when they treated her.

"Are you sure you want to see him?" Albert asked. "You couldn't have thought he was that safe to be around if he needed to wear this."

She thought of John's lips on hers, kissing her while the remote was right in her hand... Trusting her not to shock him and she, in turn, trusting him to not take the remote out of her hand.

That had been sexy and intense, but nothing compared to how she felt when he'd seen that Bobby had bitten her. Whatever feelings that had been forming between them became crystal clear when she saw the barely contained terror in his eyes when he looked at the small cut on her arm.

"I want to see him."

Albert sighed. He didn't seem remotely pleased. "If I bring you to him, will you tell me where you came from?"

Rachel blinked, frozen under this new information. John hadn't explained all that already?

Her throat started to close.

He hadn't. Rachel wasn't stupid enough to pretend that the location of her home and garden would stay secret forever, but if John hadn't said anything, it would give Matthew and the others a chance to clear it out as much as possible and get far away.

"I... I promise," she said.

She could buy some more time later. Right now, she needed to see John.

Albert nodded. "All right. Wait here. I'll call for Diane, and we'll get you something to wear."

John was losing his mind.

He stayed in the weedy grass, watching the hospital, keeping his eye on the front door. They slid open and closed as people came and went.

He recognized the cat brothers. One of whom was Sam, Charlie's mate. The pain in his heart at the sight of the guy wasn't nearly what it had once been. Sam better be taking good care of her. That was all John wanted.

Then, later, Albert and Beverly showed up. His cold

cobra heart constricted at the sight of them. They didn't have their son with them, which was good. He was probably with a babysitter. The two parents likely wanted to know where John was and wanted to speak with him. And put him back in a cage for what he'd done to them.

He stayed where he was. He'd answered Alyce Cooper's questions. Diane and Nolan had taken some notes as well then urged him to stick around, though Rachel wasn't allowed visitors at that time.

So he stayed outside, waiting. He couldn't leave Rachel there. He had to know she was all right. She would be scared for a little while. She didn't trust the people of FUC.

But they were all right. They would care for and protect her.

They'd better, anyway.

She had to be awake by now.

He waited some more. It had been two days. He'd even hunted and eaten a fresh frog earlier, filling his belly. He didn't know why no one had tried to come out and apprehended him, but he had a feeling he was being watched.

Would they capture him if he tried to slither away?

The glass doors slid open. Someone in a wheelchair was being guided out.

In his cobra form, he couldn't see colors well. Something he'd learned shortly after becoming a snake shifter. There were only blue and green corneas in his eyes.

So he couldn't see Rachel's gorgeous red hair, but it didn't take him long before he realized it was her in the wheelchair.

His heart constricted.

Albert and Diane were with her. Behind them, Beverly, Sam, and his older brother, the bobcat shifter, stood waiting.

Watching.

Albert pointed in John's general direction.

He froze.

Rachel pulled the robe tighter around her shoulders. She wore that and some slippers. John was immediately pissed. They couldn't have given her some real clothes?

She looked toward the taller grass, her eyes scanning the scene, searching for him. When Albert backed away from her wheelchair, John slithered forward, despite the fact that his biggest enemies stood so close by.

Accepting the consequences, whatever they may be.

He slithered out from his hiding place.

Rachel stopped, as though the sudden movement startled her. Had he scared her? She'd never seen him in this form before.

She looked at him, squinting her eyes just a little, then smiled, approaching him with all the familiarity of a long-time friend. The relief he felt from that alone would be worth his arrest.

She got to her knees in front of him, which couldn't be good in that pathetic little robe.

"You didn't leave."

God, his heart ached. John shifted. Fuck it. He couldn't hold back.

Rachel made a happy little sound when he was fully human and pushed herself into his arms.

"You're here," she said. "I'm so happy."

That wonderful, painful stabbing in his chest returned. He fucking loved and hated that feeling. It was too good for him.

"I wasn't gonna stay away," he assured her.

Jesus, he was naked right now, and several FUC agents were looking right at them.

"Are you okay?" Her arm was in a cast. He had no idea what it looked like underneath. "They treating you good?"

She nodded, pulling back. Her fingers were gentle when she touched his scarred face. "Albert was there when I woke up."

Albert.

John glanced back at the man over Rachel's shoulder.

"He didn't threaten you, did he?"

John didn't *think* that was the guy's M.O., but he didn't want to take a risk on that either.

She shook her head. "No, but I was worried when you weren't there. They don't have Daddy or Matthew. They asked me, but... even if I knew exactly what happened, I wouldn't tell them."

He smiled at her, a feeling of pride surging through him for her bravery. "I don't think you have to worry about the compound. I got the feeling your dad was leaving the place for good."

Her brows drew together. She didn't understand. He didn't blame her.

"Did Bobby... Did he hurt anyone else? Is Matthew okay?"

He wished he could tell her. The truth was that he had no idea where her brother was or where her father was. He just knew they weren't going to be found at the compound.

With another glance at the FUC agents behind her, John leaned in close, not wanting to give them too much information before he knew what she wanted to do. "Your brother went after TJ. I haven't seen him since. Your dad told me to get you some help, and he left."

"Right, I remember now." Rachel's eyes went wide. She didn't have the reaction he'd thought she would, however. She seemed more... resigned.

"Rachel?"

"Matthew is all right," she said, wetting her lips and nodding, as though firm in this idea. "He's strong. He can take care of himself."

"Do you know where your dad went?" John asked, fully aware that all of the people standing behind them had advanced shifter healing and could pick up every word they said.

She shook her head. "No, but... if he told you to bring me here, then he must know I was going to be safe."

She looked into John's eyes, that sadness so wide and deep he could drown in it. "You were right."

He blinked. "Right?"

"About FUC. They took care of me. Everything you said... I knew you were telling the truth. I didn't want to listen."

John ran his hands up and down her shoulders. Fuck, if he could take this pain away from her, he would. In an instant.

"TJ is missing." The words came from Albert.

John flinched then shot to his feet, pulling Rachel up with him.

Albert seemed... older, than the last time John had seen him. Like the guy hadn't been getting a lot of sleep. Two deep lines creased between his brows, like he'd been doing a lot of frowning in recent days.

Or weeks.

Seeing John again probably wasn't helping anything.

"We want to know if you have any idea where he is," Albert continued.

John shook his head, repeating the story he'd already told them when he'd first been interrogated. "I don't know anything about what happened to TJ. She doesn't either," he added. "She was poisoned, and my entire focus was on getting her help. I lost track of TJ completely."

He felt Rachel looking at the back of his head. Disappointed in him for giving everything away?

If she was, then it would be fine. He didn't like it, but it was better than them putting her into a plain room with white walls and a two-way mirror, questioning her until she gave them what they wanted.

Albert didn't seem surprised to learn of another underground compound. "There was a recent explosion. We're assuming it happened where you came from." He described the location, and it corresponded to the route that John had taken to get Rachel to FUCN'A.

"Yeah, that sounds about right."

"It was a re-purposed lab that we'd already raided. The one I'd been in." Sam spoke this time. "The explosion turned into a huge fire out there. The local fire stations struggled to keep it from turning into a wildfire."

"A fire?" John asked.

Sam nodded. "Yeah. We thought some old equipment we missed exploded. FUC is still looking into it, but maybe it was a way to... clean up evidence?"

John felt weird to be talking to the guy who mated with the woman John used to love. Mainly because he felt almost nothing at all at the sight of the man. Hard to be jealous when Rachel was right behind him and he was butt-ass naked in a deep conversation with FUC agents.

"Yeah, that's the place. Didn't you guys fill that with cement?"

"No," Albert said. "Not sure where you got that intel, but we don't do that."

"What? Why the hell not?"

"Because it takes materials FUC doesn't always have."

"How much does a few trucks of concrete cost?"

"What exactly do you think the FUC budget is?" Albert snapped back. "And why the fuck am I even arguing with you? You're the shithead that took my wife and my kid. You don't get to demand fuck all about anything we do."

Fair enough.

Albert's talons were coming out. John remembered what those felt like against his face. He didn't want to feel that again, and he definitely didn't want Rachel to see it.

"We weren't there for long," Rachel said. Everyone looked at her.

She ducked her head. Her cheeks turned a splotchy pink. Embarrassment and shame oozed from her.

"We... we moved between compounds often. Anywhere FUC hadn't found or shut down previously. I, um, don't know if you know this, but your cleanup crews leave a lot of material behind. Even when you try to cut the power, it wasn't much for us to come in and turn everything back on."

"Even so..." She seemed so unbearably sad. "It was... still home. He burned it? Everything?"

John blinked. For some reason, he'd thought Rachel had spent her whole life in that underground bunker. Spending it in multiple underground bunkers wasn't much different, he supposed, not in the grand scheme of things.

Her stuff, the little that she'd had, had been there. It was where she slept and ate. She'd clearly cared about all the flowers and everything else in her garden. Of course it would mean something to her that it was gone.

Albert was calmer when he spoke to her. "Will you talk with us? The both of you? We need to figure out what's going on. If there's someone else out there experimenting on people—"

"He's not like that," Rachel insisted. "He was trying to help us."

"To protect you from FUC?" Albert asked. "The people he ultimately sent you to?"

Rachel snapped her lips shut. She looked down, frowning, angry and helpless. John knew that feeling.

"I believe you when you say your dad isn't bad." He took her hand, keeping his voice soft, as though he were talking to a scared animal. "But you agreed with me there was something else going on. These guys just need some answers. I won't let them hurt you."

She looked at him hopefully. "Or Matthew?"

He nodded. That was an easy thing to offer. "Or Matthew."

"Your brother?" Albert asked.

Rachel nodded, her spine straightening slightly. "You would have trouble catching him anyway. He's a big, saber-toothed owl."

Albert's eyes widened. "A *what*?"

Rachel nodded, pride oozing from her. "I won't let you hurt him, but you'd have to catch him, first."

"And... he's big?" Albert asked, suspicion in his voice.

Rachel nodded. "As big as a bear. A real one. Not like me."

John grinned. Red pandas were Teddy-bear-sized.

Albert still had that strange, thoughtful expression on his face. "Right. Will you both come back inside? We can get some clothes for you, John."

He was going in with Rachel no matter what, but he had to know. "Am I under arrest?"

Albert leveled him with a steely stare. It reminded him of Matthew when the guy had been pissed off with him.

"If we were going to arrest you, Alyce would have done it

when she talked to you. We're under orders that you're a free man as long as you cooperate."

John looked back at Rachel, his decision already made. This was her first time out in the real world and her first time interacting with agents of FUC.

"I stay with her. No one gets to threaten her or scare her. Got it?"

Albert tilted his head a little and looked back at the other agents, who seemed to be hanging on the edges of their proverbial seats.

"Fine," Albert finally said. "Let's go. Get your naked ass inside before some mother with her kids sees you like that."

That was what John had asked for. It was more than he could have hoped for. Rachel's slender fingers gripped his hand tightly. She leaned in close.

One look at her, at her hopeful, if still slightly fearful, smile was enough to make John feel brave again.

Together, Rachel's hand in his, they walked back into the hospital.

20

"I have to go back." Matthew paced the little fishing cabin, furious.

With himself.

With his father.

All of it.

"Sit down." TJ had located a first-aid kit and was pulling out the meager supplies.

Matthew's face and arms had been burned to shit when the fire erupted in the compound. He'd refused to stop looking for his sister, checking the infirmary and the garden room until TJ finally convinced him that John had taken the truck and gotten her to safety.

But Matthew still grappled with the fact that his father had activated the EXIT protocol, knowing Matthew was in there.

And where the fuck were Bobby and Gerard? There had been footprints in blood.

"You need a real hospital."

"No. I'll heal," Matthew said.

He might scar.

Actually, he would scar. It was just a matter of where. His whole body throbbed. He didn't have eyebrows or eyelashes.

Or hair.

But he was alive. The cream TJ slathered on him helped.

And for some reason, he wasn't calling on FUC agents to take him away.

"I can't lie to them, about you. I have to tell them where you are," he said.

Matthew nodded. "Understood."

It was his job. Unfortunate as that was.

TJ's clothes didn't look great, but luckily, they'd only been mildly damaged due to the short amount of time TJ had burned. The fire hadn't gotten him the same way it had Matthew.

Matthew's clothes were scorched. Good for little more than rags. They smelled like burnt toast and were currently soaking in the tiny tub in the bathroom.

He would eventually put them on again when it came time to leave. He knew where his father kept some barrels buried around the compound. Money, clothes, and food would be inside... assuming he hadn't pillaged all of them after burning Matthew's home into nothing.

"Matt? You listening?"

He blinked. "Yeah, sorry. What was that?"

"Do you need more painkillers?" The guy seemed so uncomfortable. "I can... buy you some. Bring them back here for you before filing any kind of report."

Matthew smiled. "No. I'm good."

He didn't explain about the barrels. If there was a chance no one in FUC knew about them, then he wanted to keep it that way.

"Will they hurt my sister?" They'd had this discussion, too, but he needed to hear it again.

"Whether John took her to a hospital and the shifter on staff called in FUC, or John took her straight to FUCN'A, she'll be safe with them. She's probably worried about you, though."

Matthew nodded. "She will be."

He worried for her too, but John was with her. And for some reason, that reassured him.

The cobra shifter, the one who'd grabbed and kissed his sister right in front of him, was with her now. And that was better than knowing she was alone and unprotected.

John wouldn't hurt her. Matthew could accept that now.

As for FUC, he still wasn't a hundred percent on that. TJ vouched for them, and that was going to have to be enough until he could see for himself.

He sighed.

TJ didn't leave. "Say it again."

Matthew looked at him. "I swear, there was no one else down there."

"Except for Bobby and that Gerard guy?"

"Yes." He had no idea if either were alive. The bloody footprints meant *someone* had been hurt.

"And that... baby... in the tank."

"I guess."

"He wasn't experimenting on other people?"

"No." He rolled his shoulders, the healing skin tight and still burning. "Just the four of us, though I'd never actually seen anyone getting worked on, except for John when he was brought in."

His father had promised Bobby and Gerard a cure, but the two men had become convinced that it would never happen. Maybe it wouldn't have. Maybe his father never intended on helping them.

Was everything bullshit?

"You swear?"

Matthew opened his eyes, glaring at the man. "I swear."

The fox had been using Bobby and Gerard, vowing he had a cure in the works when really, he was taking care of... another child.

Another Rachel?

One of many.

Rachel Thirteen.

Many daughters.

Many attempts.

Because Rachel, Matthew's sister as he knew her, was not Bazyli's daughter.

Not his true daughter.

Matthew... was probably not related to the man in any way. Likely he was simply another pawn used for muscle— just like Bobby and Gerard had been used.

Matthew had just been more malleable since he'd lacked a memory. TJ told him that other experiments had come to FUCN'A with no memory of their pasts, so it wasn't unheard of.

So who was he?

TJ stood close. "What are you thinking about?"

"About him. My *father*. Who is not my father. Fuck, what if I..." Matthew clenched his teeth. He liked the idea of being an amnesiac more than the gnawing feeling that he was something... else. "Was I ever like that thing in that tank?"

"That seems unlikely," TJ replied. "I mean, how old are you? He couldn't have been doing all this for years without being caught."

"I was in a tank." Matthew's declaration was the truth as he remembered the pink, glowing liquid. Like a memory from a distant dream he'd forgotten.

Flashes of his time in the tank, of being cold when he came out of it, of not knowing how to describe that he was cold because he didn't have the words. Rachel hadn't taught them to him yet.

TJ's hand on Matthew's face was shocking, like a splash of cold water, waking him out of a spiral of heavy thoughts surrounding him.

TJ froze as well, as if he didn't understand why he'd done that.

They stared at each other.

Matthew felt the heat of TJ's hand through the bandages. It didn't hurt the way the heat of the fire had. His skin suddenly felt less pained.

The man really did have thick lashes.

TJ's fingers slipped away. He moved away from Matthew, toward the door, pulling it open and allowing a cold wind to enter, extinguishing the heat that had been between them.

TJ hesitated, looking back at him. "I'll tell them you and I went our separate ways, but they'll find this place eventually."

Matthew nodded, a thought occurring to him. "When you see my sister," he said, "don't tell her what you saw in Baz's office."

TJ frowned. "She's got a right to know."

Matthew clenched his fingers on the arms of the chair he sat in. He could just imagine how Rachel would take something like that. Knowing what was in that tank. Knowing she was one of many.

"I'll be the one to tell her, and I'll tell her when she's ready," he said. "It's none of your business, and she doesn't need to be worried about whether or not her father loves her or what she could do for him."

"And what about you?" TJ asked.

"What about me?"

"You're worried about what she'll think if she's alone with her thoughts. What about you? It's a lot for you to think about, too."

Matthew clenched his teeth. "I'll deal with it."

"That's it? You'll deal with it?"

Not that it was any of his business either, but if it stopped TJ from telling Rachel she might be a clone, then so be it.

"My sister took care of me and protected me when I woke up. She taught me how to speak and read. So it's my job to tell her and be there for her when she finds out. Mine. Got it?"

He expected to see pity. Or something to suggest TJ thought he was just being an idiot.

There was none of that.

Something was there, though he couldn't name it. Rachel hadn't taught him enough words, and he didn't study enough to know what that expression was on TJ's face.

"Just take care of yourself," TJ said. "That's all."

Matthew forced a smile. Felt more like a grimace. "I will. I can fly. They won't catch me."

TJ gave him a look like he wasn't impressed.

"You should only fly at night. Giant bear-sized owls get noticed, you know."

"You deal with a lot of giant shifters around here?" Matthew didn't know any. He'd only known the fox, the red panda, and the horrors that were Bobby and Gerard.

"Actually, yeah," TJ said, shocking him. "FUC has plenty of them. One woman is a giant rabbit and another a giant beaver. They both have long teeth, too."

"Hmm," Matthew said, wondering what it might be like

to meet another giant-sized shifter... and also not wanting TJ to go.

"I've got another question."

"Sure." Matthew was tired, and he knew it wasn't going to be something he'd like to answer. None of this was.

"What made you go to the Hub in the first place? Were you tired of living life underground? Looking to break away from it?"

He wanted to tell TJ that was correct, but he refused to lie. "No. I went to the Hub because I was looking for you. I wanted to bring you back to the facility and have my father examine your blood. Wanted to see if it could help in his experiments."

The moment he said it, he wondered if that was really true at all. Suddenly, it sounded to his own ears like it had been an excuse and that TJ's reasoning made more sense. Matthew had become restless. Had wanted to break out...

But it was too late. TJ snarled at him. His face twisted to something vile.

He left the cabin, slamming the door shut behind him.

It was quiet, by himself. Matthew wished he could explain, but there probably wasn't anything he could have said that would have made this any better.

His father was gone, probably someone who couldn't even be his true kin. Rachel was likely being treated by FUC agents, but she at least had John with her, and TJ... well, Matthew wouldn't be practicing his reading by texting the man anymore.

At least he had the pain of his burns to keep him company. The healing caused a tingling that was both hot and cold at the same time. Time would tell how much scarring he'd have by the end of it.

He'd rest here a little while longer.

21

Rachel wasn't used to having so many people around. She wasn't used to having to answer questions from those people either. Her father always asked the questions. He was the one she had to listen to.

He was the one who knew what to do, how to keep her safe and fed and warm.

Until he wasn't there anymore. Until she had to accept that her father wasn't who he said he was. That he might, in fact, have been doing bad things.

Not small-scale bad things either, like when he asked Rachel and Matthew to steal documents for him.

Big bad things.

After another day in the hospital, she was informed that the poison had run its course. Her arm had been saved, and so had her life. Her shifter healing had taken control and worked with the medicine she'd been given.

Her arm was scarred, as though the poison Bobby had put inside her ate away at her flesh, leaving a long, ugly canyon of skin where that simple little scratch had been.

At least her arm still worked, even though it felt weak, but that was all.

She was asked to transform into her red panda shape a couple of times and walk around, allowing the doctors to assess the damage.

She couldn't walk on all fours without limping, without feeling like her arm was about to give out under her weight.

She couldn't climb anything either.

She hated it.

John had looked at her with sympathy in his eyes she absolutely had not wanted, the both of them sitting on her hospital bed while waiting to be released.

Then he kissed the ruined flesh and looked her in the eyes.

"You're beautiful."

That caught her breath

Of course, he was lying. He couldn't be telling the truth, but... for a few, brief seconds, she forgot about it.

Just a few.

"It's not nice to look at."

"Well, what do you think about these?"

He pointed to the scars on his face.

She cringed. "That's... different. You still look good."

She blushed.

He looked handsome. Always did. She couldn't picture him without the scars.

He choked out a soft laugh. "Right, sorry, I forgot. Chicks dig scars."

"They do?" She hadn't known that.

He nodded. "Yup. And I happen to think you're still gorgeous." He kissed her mark again. "You had to live to get this. I fucking love you for that."

A small choked sound escaped her throat.

"Why'd you have to go and say that?"

She lunged at him, kissing John again and again on her hospital bed.

He'd said he loved her.

He said he loved me.

Rachel was over the moon. She didn't have the words to describe the intensity of the feeling surging through her. It felt electric, uncontainable, and eager to spill out in any way it could.

More kisses seemed to be the best way to handle that.

She would have pushed herself into his lap, would have slid her hands under his shirt, had one of the doctors, Diane, not shown up and guided them out of the hospital wing.

Along with several other FUC agents.

It was time to go.

They had been given clothes. Rachel's dress had been cut off her when she'd been unconscious. She was sad that it was gone but excited for something different to wear. The jeans, tank top, and plaid shirt felt strange.

She almost felt normal... if she could remember what normal was.

Everything happened in a whirl after that.

They were put in the back of a van, but the windows were not blacked out, as though they were in trouble. The shifter named Steve was driving, while Albert and Sam spoke to them in the back seat.

As if they were guests.

"You're going to be under observation for a while," Albert said, passing Rachel a yellow folder.

Inside was... nothing nefarious.

It was a photo of a small cottage. Pictures of the inside. It seemed warm and cozy, the exact opposite of what she was used to. What she thought she could have.

Flowers grew outside. Not like the ones she'd been growing, which she had told them about. There had been no point in hiding that detail after everything was destroyed.

"FUC gives this to its prisoners?" She suddenly felt a new wave of guilt over the cage John had been trapped in for the first several days of his stay with her.

"No," Albert said. "This is more of a special circumstance sort of situation. You have information we need, and John is hardly off the hook, but he did negotiate your accommodations well."

Albert sounded as though he were reluctant to give that compliment.

This was because of John?

When they finally arrived, they were given a tour of the simple, one-bedroom cabin. The bedroom being the loft above the open-concept kitchen and living room.

The bathroom was clean and luxurious, which had a standing shower with nice, new tiles. There were no stalls she would be expected to share with Matthew, Bobby, or Gerard.

Just John.

"Sorry it's not a lot," Sam said, as if it wasn't perfectly lovely. "There are cameras outside, watching this place closely. FUC agents will know if either of you tries leaving."

"How would they watch John?" she asked. Snakes were smaller and easier to miss if they wanted to hide

John scratched the back of his head. "I won't be shifting for a while, Rachel."

She blinked, not understanding, a slight panic building within her. "What?"

"Part of his deal with us," Albert said, giving her a set of keys.

She noticed they did that. Anything physical that was handed over, keys or papers, were all given to her. As though Albert wanted to avoid John in all instances. Even when it came to handing him the keys to the cabin.

"What deal?"

"It's not a big deal. The treatment is similar to what your dad had me on. It's just so they can keep an eye on me."

Her heart lurched. "Is it... permanent?"

The reminder of her father's warning, how agents of FUC would try to remove her shifting ability, rushed back to her. They'd done it to John.

"No," Albert said. "But we'll be around from time to time to make sure he's topped up on the dosage and to check his tracker."

"Tracker?"

John sighed, lifting his pant leg, and showing her the device that was around his ankle.

Her throat closed. This wasn't what she wanted. She didn't want John to be a prisoner again.

He grabbed her shoulders. "It's okay. Hey, look at me. It's fine."

"They're... they..."

"They're doing what they have to do, because I'm still a criminal, and I need to pay for that," he said, with all the calm certainty and authority of a man who knew what needed to be done and was going to do it come hell or high water.

"But—"

"I suggested it," John said. "And it doesn't seem like such a bad idea to me. As long as I don't put up a fuss, you and I can stay in this nice little place. We still answer some questions, and they go easy on you about the compound."

"Will they... will they try to take away my red panda?"

The thought was horrifying. She'd been willing to risk her father's wrath from time to time to let it out, to climb trees and play in her other shape. If these people were going to take it away, then she didn't want this stupid cabin no matter how pretty it was.

"No, that was never on the table," Albert said.

"How do I know that?" she snapped, hating Albert, having no patience for the way he was treating John.

"You might have information we need because you're the daughter of a dangerous man, but we don't punish the children of our suspects. Not without proof of involvement."

"It's okay." John stroked her arms, leaning in close, whispering, "I wanted this, Rachel."

She looked at him. Into his sincere eyes. A pleading was so obviously there, along with the desperate need to make up for his past wrongs.

He'd said he wanted to help her, to make her see that her father wasn't exactly who he said he was. He'd done that then saved her life by rushing her to the hospital.

It just occurred to Rachel there were some things she would not be able to heal for him. Some things he needed to do himself to cleanse his soul.

She gave in, though it didn't feel good. "All right."

It was as if there was a collective sigh of relief. Steve continued to show her around the cabin, where the TV was, the remote, and how to use it, as if she wouldn't know.

Then it was out to the gardens, with the promise she could be out in them whenever she wanted. She could even shift into her panda form for exercise but was warned to not leave the property.

There was a lake not too far away where all the aquatic cadets studied, but she could apparently go swimming there, too.

"Swimming will be fun, right?" Even John seemed excited. "And you can grow so many flowers here. Look at these beds!"

He was determined that she should see this as a good thing.

Rachel decided it would be. For his sake, she would be happy here, but on one condition.

"You promise you're staying here with me?"

He seemed shocked, and a little embarrassed, by the request. "Only if you want me to. These guys are offering this for you. I think Albert wouldn't mind seeing me in a cage again."

"I would rather he didn't do that, so, yes, I'd like you here with me."

His confession of love still burned in her chest, like a log feeding a nice, warm fire.

John brought her hand to his mouth, kissing the knuckles when Sam and Albert weren't looking.

Outside, Steve honked the horn, clearly done with waiting around for them.

"Call this number if you ever need anything," Sam said, giving her a steady look. "We agreed to this and are doing it because he brought you to the hospital, and you're giving the all clear for him to be here, but if at any point you change your mind or don't feel safe with him—"

"That won't happen," Rachel said, looping her arms around John's, holding him tight. Closer. "I'm safe with him."

She felt John stand two inches taller at her certainty.

The FUC agents took their leave.

It was a little strange, being so close to the Academy whose bins she used to snoop around in. God, she would never be able to see them again without cringing.

Oh well.

"So, this place is nice, eh?"

"Yes," Rachel said, getting an idea in her head and pulling him to the steep little staircase.

"I'd like to see the loft. They didn't show us up there."

John got an interested look on his face, and with a slight thrill in her belly, Rachel realized that John might just know what she was going to ask him for.

They went up.

The ceiling was low up top.

Rachel could stand at her full height, but John just barely, the ceiling just an inch away from the top of his head.

There was a skylight above the bed, which Rachel was definitely excited about.

"I've always wanted to sleep under the stars," she said. "This is going to be amazing."

"Yeah," John said, looking only at her.

Heat crawled up Rachel's neck. Her whole body felt warm. Her whole body felt good.

She hadn't lied when she told Sam and Albert how safe she felt with John, but it was odd to think of how true it really was.

And how quickly it had happened.

Rachel pulled off her shirt.

"Whoa," John said, stopping her immediately.

"You don't want to?"

"I mean..." He laughed a little. "Christ, *yes*, I want to, but I didn't want to push you, seeing as how I'm your first kiss and everything."

"First kiss I can remember," she said, a little sad to let him in on the revelation she'd had. "I think I have done this before, but it's hard to say."

She pulled off the plaid shirt, then the tank top, dropping them both and standing there in the jeans and black sports bra she'd been given.

"I'd like to... with you... if you want to, but it's okay if you don't—"

John rushed to her, his mouth on hers before she could ramble on any more than that.

He kissed her like she would disappear from his arms if he stopped.

It was exactly the way she wanted to be kissed. The press of his mouth against hers, claiming her, was wonderful.

But even Rachel had to take a breath.

They pulled back from each other with a short gasp, looking at each other, as though waiting for... something.

"I wanna do something for you," John said, pushing her down onto the bed and unbuttoning her jeans. She helped him to get them down, feeling a little greedy but also eager to know what he wanted to do.

"You've already done so much for me."

"One more thing," he said, a wicked grin pulling at his lips. "You're gonna like this. I promise."

Her underwear went next. Rachel reached for him, wanting to pull his body on top of hers, but he knelt down lower between her legs instead.

And then kissed her... *there*.

Rachel almost flew off the bed, as though a match had been lit under her ass.

At first, his kiss was gentle, and even that was enough to send shockwaves rippling over every inch of her skin. Her whole body was affected.

And when his tongue licked at the folds of her sex, pushing inside...

Rachel was done for. Her hands came over her mouth, her spine bowing as she struggled to hold back any noise.

Just because the others had left didn't mean she wanted to take the risk of someone hearing her.

God, she almost didn't care.

When she blinked and came to, John was above her, staring down at her, an expression on his face that was something between a proud grin and disbelief.

"That was wonderful," she said, her whole body humming with pleasure.

John laughed. "I'm glad you liked it. I want to make it last a little while longer for you next time."

"Sorry," she said quickly.

He kissed her jaw, her neck, and then her collarbone, shaking his head. "Don't be." His short laugh and a puff of cool air against her skin gave her goosebumps. "Strokes my ego real nice knowing I can do that to you."

Speaking of stroking things...

Rachel reached down between them. His cock was hard. She could feel it through his jeans the same way she'd felt it that second time he'd kissed her.

Kissed her and she'd done nothing about it.

He had to be suffering.

"I want to make you feel good," she said, so eager, knowing what she had to do and executing her plan.

Rachel pushed herself up, grabbing his shoulders and, with a strength that shocked even her, flung him down onto the bed.

John didn't seem to mind. He looked eager.

"I think I like this side of you."

"Yeah?" she asked quietly.

John pushed himself up, kissing her mouth softly. "I like all sides of you," he said. "I mean it."

She loved him.

She was so, so in love with him that it scared her.

But just as she now belonged to him, there was a responsibility in knowing he also belonged to her. She vowed to always act wisely with that knowledge and to care for him, in every way he cared for her.

She pushed herself down his legs, getting to his knees, pulling his jeans with her as she went. She was suddenly very glad she and John had this private place, all to themselves.

She took John's cock into her hand, giving it a gentle stroke.

John closed his eyes, his lips pressing together. A soft noise escaped his throat. She looked up at him, pleased when he finally looked back at her, and holding that eye contact, Rachel kissed the length of his dick, the shaft pulsing softly beneath her lips.

John's mouth dropped open as he watched her, refusing to close his eyes for long as she worked.

"*Fuuuuck*, Rachel, I—"

Now it was her turn to expertly cut him off as, in one neat, clean motion, she took the length of him, as much as she could fit, into her mouth.

Rachel tried to go all the way but quickly learned her skills did not reach that far.

Rachel had to pull back, irritated with herself, but that was a feeling she easily shoved away because of the sounds John made.

He didn't seem to mind that she couldn't fit his whole cock into her mouth, and he seemed extra delighted when she used her hand to stroke the skin she couldn't get to, so she did that instead.

"Fuck, Rachel, baby," he moaned. His thick fingers pushed in and out of her hair, as though torn between holding on or giving her the space she needed to move at her own pace.

She wouldn't mind it if he would hold on to the back of her head, but in the end, she decided this was a good enough pace for now.

They would get there. There was so much time for them to do whatever they wanted to do, to learn about each other, and to pleasure each other.

They would get there.

Gently taking John's tight testicles in her hand seemed like a good idea, softly. Carefully massaging them while hollowing her cheeks had the desired effect.

John came with a shout, falling back onto the sheets in a boneless pile.

He looked down at her, blinking blearily, as though blinking away stars.

Rachel made sure to stare back at him as she swallowed down everything he gave her. John's eyes widened, his dick somehow pulsing again, as though trying to get hard again right away.

"Christ, come up here. Right now."

She did, easily sliding into his arms so he could hold her, kiss her, and stroke her.

They made love on and off, resting between rounds.

Rachel hadn't known she could have that sort of energy. Or that John could, for that matter.

She was impressed.

"How do you feel?"

She grinned, looking away from the night sky and stars that shone through the skylight.

They had been in bed for a while.

"I don't remember my other times, but I know they weren't anything like that."

"Oh yeah?" He nudged her. "How can you tell?"

Rachel curled herself against him, pleased and satisfied as his arm settled around her. "I just know."

John chuckled, his nose suddenly in her hair, his thumb stroking back and forth across her shoulder.

"I've got a bad idea," he said.

"What is it?"

"Well..." He sighed. "It's nighttime, and it's late enough that I don't think anyone will come across us, but..." He looked at her, that mischief back on his face. "I'm thinking I wanna go skinny-dipping in the FUCN'A lake. Christen it, so to speak."

Rachel had no idea who she was. She never would have agreed to something like that before. Right now, though...

"I'll race you there!" she shouted, jumping out of bed and rushing down the stairs.

They stopped for shoes and towels and that was it before they raced to the lake.

Rachel wanted to shift, to race him as her panda, but that wouldn't be fair, even with her weak arm.

If he couldn't shift, she wouldn't either, for as long as she could get away with, anyway. Maybe, just maybe, she could convince Albert, and the rest of FUC, that John wasn't a flight risk. That just because he was a snake, a cobra, it didn't make him evil.

Then they could shift together. Play together.

For now, the night was theirs.

The End

NOT QUITE! There are more FUC Academy books coming your way soon, and plenty for you to go back and enjoy!

To find out more about these books and more, visit Worlds.EveLanglais.com or sign up for the EveL Worlds newsletter. If you haven't already downloaded the **free Academy intro** (written by Eve Langlais) make sure you grab it at worlds.evelanglais.com/wordpress/book/fucacademy1!

FIERCE FLEDGLINGS BY MANDY ROSKO

In these four books by Mandy Rosko, a mysterious villain and her snake son are stirring up trouble around the Furry United Coalition Newbie Academy, but a menagerie of FUC agents will stop at nothing to thwart them, and protect the ones they love!

I'll Be Dammed

Albert makes Beverly feel safe, though she has no memory of her mate or her life before someone kidnapped her and did freaky science things to her.

Trash Queen

FUCN'A won't release Trisha into "normal" society until she's able to hide the large horn protruding from her forehead. The new security guard catches her stealing, and captures her heart in the process.

Chillin' Out

Charlie wishes she could remember her life before the lab. Especially when a cobra shows up in her room, and claims they used to have a life together. But she's pretty sure she' supposed to be with a certain cat—the new and overly protective FUCN'A security guard!

Bits and Bobs

Steve's little trip to BC to help his brother turned into more than he bargained for when a strange bird-woman abducted him. Now all of a sudden he can turn into some kind of cat... what?!!

ABOUT THE AUTHOR

USA Today Bestselling Author Mandy Rosko is a videogame playing, book loving chick. She loves writing paranormal romances that range from light steamy to erotic, and has some contemporary and historical romances as well. You can find her on all sorts of platforms, including Twitch, where she does writing sprints, crafting, and video gaming!

Get all the latest news from Mandy by signing up for her newsletter: https://www.subscribepage.com/mandyrosko

Lightning Source UK Ltd.
Milton Keynes UK
UKHW010736200123
415680UK00001B/204